Everyone loves Sammy Keyes!

"A fitting tribute to Sammy."
—*School Library Journal*

"The sleuth delights from start to finish."
—*Publishers Weekly*

"A high-quality, high-amp mystery series."
—*The Horn Book*

"An intelligent, gutsy, flawed, and utterly likable heroine."
—*Booklist*

"Sammy Keyes comes armed with attitude."
—*Orlando Sentinel*

"Van Draanen offers such an explosive combination of
high-stakes sleuthing, hilarity, and breathlessly paced
action that it's impossible to turn the pages fast enough."
—*Kirkus Reviews*

"Sammy Keyes is the hottest sleuth to appear
in children's books since Nancy Drew."
—*The Boston Globe*

"Sammy doesn't find mysteries to solve—they find her."
—*Arizona Republic*

"The only thing better than a good mystery
is a good mystery series."
—*Teacher*

Also by Wendelin Van Draanen

How I Survived Being a Girl

Flipped

Swear to Howdy

Runaway

Confessions of a Serial Kisser

The Running Dream

The Secret Life of Lincoln Jones

Wild Bird

WENDELIN VAN DRAANEN

SAMMY KEYES

AND THE Kiss Goodbye

A Yearling Book

This is a work of fiction. Names, characters, places, and incidents either are the product of the author's imagination or are used fictitiously. Any resemblance to actual persons, living or dead, events, or locales is entirely coincidental.

Visit us on the Web! rhcbooks.com

Educators and librarians, for a variety of teaching tools, visit us at RHTeachersLibrarians.com

Grateful acknowledgment is made to the following for permission to reprint previously published material: Alfred Publishing: Excerpt from "The Teddy Bears' Picnic," words by Jimmy Kennedy, music by John W. Bratton, copyright © 1947 (Renewed) by WB Music Corp. and EMI Music Publishing LTD. All rights administered by WB Music Corp. Reprinted by permission of Alfred Publishing.

Library of Congress Cataloging-in-Publication Data is available upon request.

ISBN 978-0-307-93063-7 (pbk.) — ISBN 978-0-307-97410-5 (ebook)

Printed in the United States of America

10 9 8 7 6 5 4 3 2 1

First Yearling Edition 2018

Random House Children's Books supports the First Amendment and celebrates the right to read.

For Sammy,
who has taught me so much

SAMMY KEYES

AND THE Kiss Goodbye

A WARNING FROM WENDELIN

Let me start by saying I'm sorry.

I know you were expecting Sammy.

I know you were looking forward to her telling you all about some madcap escapade that had her braving short-cuts or snooping through basements or ditching bad guys.

Or cops.

I know you're here to laugh and race along with her as she gets into scrapes and trouble and finally finds her way back home.

She would be here if she could, but . . . she can't. And since everyone else is either too busy trying to help or having too much trouble dealing to let you know what's going on, you're stuck with me.

I'm having a lot of trouble, too, believe me. But I thought you should know. As hard as it is to hear, as much as it hurts to tell, you deserve to know what's happened to Sammy Keyes.

1—WEDNESDAY NIGHT

Holly is the one who found her.

There was a lot of screaming.

And crying.

And as we all know, Holly is not a screamer. Or a crier. But afterward people said that her wails surely woke the dead.

Unfortunately, they did not wake Sammy Keyes.

Holly saw the whole thing—or, at least, parts of the whole thing—and when Sergeant Borsch found *that* out, he became relentless. (Or, as Sammy would have said, like a dog with a bone.)

"From the beginning," he commanded Holly as he pulled her into a chair in the emergency room. "Every detail."

Despite his tough-cop exterior, Sergeant Gilbert Borsch was, at the moment, a gun-slinging puddle of misery, his face etched deep with a single burning question:

Who did this?

(Well, there were other questions forming lines among those already present from years on the force—questions like Why? and When? and Where? and How? But the deepest, most painful crease was caused by the fiery rage of Who?)

Holly wasn't focused on Sergeant Borsch or his topographic face. She stared instead at the door through which Sammy's stretcher had been wheeled, and whimpered, "Is she going to be all right?"

Sergeant Borsch sucked on a tooth (an infamous habit cultivated before his doctor had suggested he quit with the pastrami and take up with turkey). Then he gruffed, "I'm not a doctor," which was cop code for No, or Probably not, or Don't get your hopes up—the latter being something Sergeant Borsch had learned was safer for his heart than optimism.

Or, regrettably, pastrami.

But suddenly Holly's adoptive mother, Meg Talbrook, was blasting through the door, wrapping Holly in her arms as she panted out incoherent phrases and fragmented clauses and hopelessly dangling modifiers.

And since Meg was a dog groomer, which was just *thiiiis* far away from being a veterinarian, which (as everyone suspects but won't actually say) is just *thiiiis* far away from being a doctor, and since there were, at that time, no doctors in attendance, Holly looked at her mother with desperate puppy-dog eyes and begged, "Tell me she's going to be all right."

The fragmented clauses suddenly ceased, Meg's shoulders squared back, and her solid frame jelled into a protective barrier between her daughter and reality. Then she held her daughter's face in her hands and lied with the unwavering conviction only a parent in crisis can muster. "She's going to be fine."

"It's bad, Mom. There was a lot of blood. She wouldn't wake up. She wouldn't . . . she was just . . ."

"Who are we dealing with here, *hmm*?" Meg asked, sitting beside her. "Have you ever known anyone to get the better of Sammy?" She lifted Holly's chin. "She was breathing, right? Her heart was beating, right?"

"I don't know! They put a mask on her and stuck tubes in her and told me to stay back."

Meg cast a wary eye on Sergeant Borsch, silently asking what he might know of the situation, but the best the Borschman could seem to do was, "She wasn't under a white sheet. That's all I know."

"Don't you have connections?" Meg whispered. "Can't you find out?"

"They'll come out when they know something," the lawman stated. "That's how this works. Me demanding information is gonna get us nothin' but stonewalled. What I need to find out, ma'am, is who did this. That's *my* job, and I really need your daughter's cooperation."

Meg turned to Holly, who looked down to collect her thoughts, but instead got caught up thinking about her shoes.

They were high-tops, just like Sammy's.

It used to be just Sammy who wore high-tops, but now a lot of kids at William Rose Junior High did. Even (to the administration's chagrin) some of the teachers. It was just one of those *things*. Something Sammy had started, not by trying, but by just standing up and *being*.

"Holly?" Sergeant Borsch rasped. "Holly, please."

But instead of coming out with who, what, where, when, or why, what Holly said was, "She saved my life, you know. That time at the riverbed? When that creep was coming after me? She took him down with her umbrella."

"That big black thing?" Meg asked. "You never told me that!"

"Please," Sergeant Borsch said again, desperate for them to discuss the past in the *future,* not now, when he was trying to deal with the present.

Holly took a deep, choppy breath, held it for a moment, then said, "She was on her way home—"

"Home?" Sergeant Borsch asked. "But that makes no sense! This happened at the Highrise!"

As you're probably aware, Sergeant Borsch is not known for his tact or his patience. And although he *is* a more tactful and patient man now than he was as a street-beat officer when Sammy first met him, these characteristics would need major work should he ever aspire to reach the rank of lieutenant. Or captain. Or (pray for the City of Santa Martina) chief.

So it came as no surprise to Holly that after just one short sentence Sergeant Borsch had already interrupted her, but Meg was not so accustomed to the lawman's brusque ways. "The girls had been studying for exams," she began.

"At the Pup Parlor?" Sergeant Borsch interjected, again interrupting after a single sentence.

"At our apartment above the business," Meg said. "It was after nine and dark outside. I was heading off to take a shower before bed and told Sammy she should get home before her grandmother began to worry."

"But her grandmother no longer lives in the Highrise!"

Sergeant Borsch's confusion was understandable. Not so long ago Sammy had lived illegally with her grandmother on the fifth floor of Santa Martina's only government-subsidized housing for seniors—the Senior Highrise (clearly named in a moment of unrivaled creative genius).

And although the secret of Sammy's residence had never been openly discussed, the Borschman had figured it out and immediately wished he hadn't. How could he let this girl continue to sneak up and down the fire escape and sleep on her grandmother's couch when doing so was against the law?

It was the first time in his career that Officer Borsch had consciously looked the other way, convincing himself that there were bigger wrongs in this world than a kid sleeping on an old lady's couch.

Still, no one was more relieved than Gil Borsch when Sammy's grandmother married the straight-shooting Hudson Graham, and the lawbreakers and their cat took up legal residence with the septuagenarian on Cypress Street.

But that move had occurred months earlier, which is why (despite his abrasive demeanor and propensity for interruption) it was legitimate for an investigating officer to ask, "What was Sammy doing at the Highrise?"

And ask it he did.

Holly's head quivered side to side. "She said something about the Nightie-Napper."

The creases in Sergeant Borsch's face deepened.

Especially the ones above and between his eyebrows. Entire rivers could have coursed through them without hazarding overflow. "The Nightie-Napper?"

Holly nodded. "It bugged her that she never figured out who the Nightie-Napper was."

"So this . . . this *Nightie-Napper* did this to her?"

"No!" Holly's head quivering resumed. "At least I don't think so!"

Again, it was Meg who came to the rescue. "Holly, sweetheart," she said with a soothing voice, "we don't understand what you're talking about. Explain what a nightie-napper is."

"The Nightie-Napper has been stealing stuff out of the dryers in the basement at the Highrise. They've been doing it for a long time."

"Stuff?" Meg prompted. "Like . . . nightgowns?"

Holly shrugged. "And muumuus."

"Muumuus," Sergeant Borsch moaned. "What has this—"

Since Meg was a woman of both internal and external substance, it took a simple STOP hand signal for her to shut him down. Then she continued coaxing information from her obviously traumatized daughter. "Is the Nightie-Napper someone you think might try to kill a fourteen-year-old girl?"

Holly's eyes pinched closed. "The Nightie-Napper doesn't have anything to do with this!"

Sergeant Borsch's hands flew skyward. "Then why are you—"

STOP went Meg's hand again. And like a Rottweiler warning off an intruder, she locked eyes with him and bared her teeth ever so slightly as she growled, "She'll get to it."

And after a little head bobbing and recollecting and sorting and thinking, Holly did indeed get to it. "Sammy talked about the Nightie-Napper. She also wondered if her gum was still in the fire-escape doorjamb. She was trying to picture what the new neighbor was like. Her name's Violet, and Sammy thought that was strange."

"Why strange?" Meg asked, but then with a laugh she got it. "Oh! First Daisy, then Rose, now Violet!"

"Exactly." Holly took a deep breath, then continued. "It seemed like she missed the place. I told her she should take me there someday, because I'd never been inside, and after all the stories she'd told, I really wanted to sneak up the fire escape and peek down the hallway and hide out in the basement and maybe catch the Nightie-Napper red-handed."

Now, an ordinary parent might have filed this particular conversation away in her mental To Be Discussed folder, but Meg was no ordinary parent. She had taken the runaway Holly in, saving her from a life of homelessness, and no sleuthing adventure through a seniors building would (or could) come close to the dangers Holly had already faced.

Besides, this wasn't about going places you shouldn't.

This was about Sammy.

So Meg simply waited for Holly to continue, needing

9

to employ only one STOP signal to quell Sergeant Borsch's questions before Holly's focus returned.

"After she left, I watched her through the window. She rode her skateboard up to Main Street and crossed Broadway. Only when she got to the other side, she didn't cross again and go toward Hudson's the way she always does. She just stood looking over at the Highrise for a little while. Then she rode down Main and disappeared into the bushes like she used to when she lived at the Highrise."

Meg asked her daughter a question that Gil Borsch would never in a million years have thought to ask: "Did that upset you?"

Holly's head bobbed. "Yes! I'd *just* talked to her about wanting to go there with her—why couldn't she wait for sometime when I could go, too?"

"So you watched to see if she really was going up the fire escape?"

"Yes! And she did! And at first I was really mad!"

"But then?"

"But then I saw someone start up the stairs after her."

"And . . . ?"

"And . . . and they were moving fast. Like they were chasing her. I called her cell phone to warn her, but her phone started ringing in our kitchen! So I opened the window and yelled for her to watch out, but that was hopeless because of the traffic. And then there was a big struggle and I saw Sammy fall off the fire escape." Holly's eyes welled with tears. "It was the third floor, Mom. Nobody can survive that."

"There were bushes," Meg assured her.

Even in that moment Holly recognized the irony of Meg's statement. Bushes had been a big part of Sammy's duck-and-cover routine. Bushes had concealed her from foes and cops alike. Bushes had been her primary spy spot, and once again, she had landed in them.

Only this wasn't funny.

Not funny at all.

But pondering the irony of bushes provided a silence and, consequently, a long-awaited entry into the conversation for Sergeant Borsch. "How would you describe this person who followed Sammy up the stairs?" he asked. "Tall? Short? Thin? Hefty?"

Holly thought a moment, then shook her head. "Kind of medium."

If there's one answer Sergeant Borsch has been known to ridicule, it's "kind of medium." But this time it didn't seem to even register on his finely calibrated annoyance meter, and he just went on. "Man? Woman?"

Holly hesitated. "I figured it was a man, but . . . but . . . I guess it *could* have been a woman."

"Hair? Clothing?"

"It was dark! I don't know!"

"Where did the assailant go? Up? Down?"

"I don't know! I saw Sammy fall and I screamed and called 911!"

"How'd you know it was Sammy falling and not the other person?"

"Her backpack! She was wearing her backpack!"

The three of them sat there, Holly in tears, Meg trying to comfort her, and Sergeant Borsch numbed to the core.

He had nothing.

Nothing to work with.

Not a single clue.

2—THE SWINGING DOOR OF (MAYBE) DEATH

News travels fast in the digital age, and not long after Holly smacked Sergeant Borsch with the one-two punch of Don't Know and Not Sure, teenagers started coming through the emergency-room door.

The first one on the scene was Heather Acosta.

"Where is she?" she panted, looking around wildly as if Sammy were her best friend, instead of the girl she'd tortured and *wished* dead for well over a year.

Holly groaned at the sight of her. She was not (and would likely never be) convinced that Heather was sincere in her newfound enthusiasm for Sammy. And despite Sammy's willingness to let bygones be bygones, Holly was not one to forget Heather Acosta's long history of deceit and revenge (not to mention brazen backstabbing). It was hard for her to believe that three "shell-shocking" days in Las Vegas had really changed Heather.

But there Heather was, gasping and gushing concern, her red hair flashing like a squad-car light as she spun around, searching for Sammy. "She's not . . . ," she said, her voice trailing off as she cast her wide eyes on Holly, Meg, and Sergeant Borsch.

And since Holly, Meg, and Sergeant Borsch each held similar suspicions about Heather, none of them jumped up with assurances that Sammy would be all right. They simply stared.

What this lack of assurance triggered in Heather was a crumpling at the knees and a scream so fierce and pathetic and *loud* that emergency-room personnel began appearing to see if anyone was being stabbed in the waiting room (something that was, unfortunately, not unheard of at Santa Martina's Community Hospital).

"Stop it!" Holly shouted at Heather. "We don't know anything yet!"

But Heather was folded into herself on the floor, so deafened by her own primal wailing that she didn't hear what Holly was saying.

And then Casey Acosta came blasting in and saw (and heard) his sister wailing on the floor, which immediately set him falling into the same pit of despair as his life with Sammy flashed before his eyes.

The tortured look on his face could have broken the heart of Death himself. If Death was around. Which nobody really knew at that point. (Although in the emergency room the odds were alarmingly high.)

What Casey's reaction *did* do was kick Holly into gear. "No one's said she's dead yet!" Holly shouted, jumping out of her seat. "They're still working on her!"

This did a nice job of shutting Heather up, but it didn't happen fast enough for Nurse Cathy Abbey, who came ramming through the main interior door, shouting, "You need to SHUT UP out here!" Her pants were a tired blue, her shoes a scuffed white, and the geometric designs on her smock were a telling sign of her impersonal approach to patient care.

"Is there any news?" Holly asked.

"When there's news, we'll tell ya!" Nurse Abbey snapped, then withdrew through the emergency room's swinging door of fate.

"So she's not . . . ?" Heather asked, looking up from her crumpled position on the floor.

"We don't know!" Holly snapped, and then to her enormous relief, Marissa McKenze rushed in from outside, followed almost immediately by Billy Pratt.

Marissa and Billy were tried-and-true friends. Maybe not with each other, seeing how Marissa had dumped Billy for the smooth-talking Danny Urbanski, breaking Billy's heart for at least a week. But Billy and Marissa had been through the thick of things with Sammy, and that's what mattered now.

"What's *she* doing here?" Marissa seethed after Holly had given all of them a quick recap. Like Holly, Marissa trusted Heather about as far as she could throw a tiger. "And who is she texting?"

"She's not just texting," Holly said, craning a little to see better. "She's posting."

"What? No! Tell her to stop! We don't want a bunch of people here!"

But the reality was, neither Holly nor Marissa knew how to tell Heather to stop. The only person who seemed to be able to reason with Heather was Sammy . . . and sometimes Casey.

But Casey was fighting back tears as he whispered with Billy, and Marissa didn't have the heart to interrupt their conversation to ask him to deal with something she could do herself. Even though she couldn't.

Meg had noted Heather's flurry of phone activity, too, and saw a different sort of downside. She leaned over and asked Sergeant Borsch, "Does Sammy's grandmother know what's happened?" The question was met with the blank look of a man in shock, so she added, "Rita's the guardian—I'm sure they'll need her here. And someone really should tell her before the rumor mill does." Then, since the lawman still seemed too stunned to take action, she offered, "If you have her number, I could call her."

Gil Borsch did, in fact, have the number, but even through the daze of his despair, he knew this was not the sort of thing he should break to Rita over the phone. So he pulled himself together and stood, saying, "I'll tell her in person." Then he gave his cell number to Meg so she could call him if there were any developments and hauled his heavy heart outside.

On the short ride over to Cypress Street, it occurred to Sergeant Borsch that he was the very worst person for this job. Since the facts were sketchy and the outcome uncertain, he didn't know what to say. The situation was gray on gray, and Gil Borsch worked best when things were black on white.

So he called his wife. However, instead of acknowledging that he really needed to talk to somebody, he convinced himself he was doing it because she would want to know. After all, Deb was a huge fan of Sammy's. She'd even asked Sammy to be a bridesmaid in their wedding! Never mind that Sammy had almost *ruined* the wedding with one of her daredevil escapades—that was beside the point. Deb loved her and would want to know.

Plus, he could try this breaking-the-news thing out on her.

Unfortunately, it did not go well.

Not due to Deb's reaction.

Due to his.

Besides breaking down while breaking the news, Gil Borsch also broke the hands-free law while making the call—something he'd been quick to ticket other drivers for doing.

So after hanging up, he felt both broken up *and* dirty—worse off by far than he'd been before he'd made the call. But as awful as he felt (and as raw and red as his eyes now looked), he was already at the Cypress Street residence, and really, there was no turning back from duty. Especially since Rita and Hudson were both sitting on the porch, presumably waiting for Sammy's postcurfew return.

Sergeant Borsch appearing at the Cypress Street residence (either via squad car or in his personal vehicle, which he now drove) was not, in and of itself, cause for concern for Hudson or Rita. The two had grown to know (and even like) the lawman, especially since he seemed to keep a weather eye out for Sammy and had delivered her home safely from one tangle or another more often than they cared to recall.

This time, however, neither the front nor back passenger door of Gil Borsch's car swung open.

This time, no skateboard or backpack or high-tops emerged.

This time, Hudson was the first to realize, something was wrong.

"Sergeant?" he called, hurrying down the porch steps as Rita followed closely behind.

So, with a fumbling of words and barely checked emotions, Sergeant Borsch managed to convey the crucial points:

Sammy was hurt.

Badly hurt.

They needed to get to the hospital.

Now.

Old people are not known for their quick movements. But these two seniors became instant Olympic contenders, dashing and leaping and propelling into the house and out again as they snatched up keys and cash and insurance cards and dived into the Borschman's car without invitation.

Gil Borsch just went with it. He jumped in behind the wheel, slapped his portable spinning light onto the roof, and gunned it back to the hospital.

The car was still rolling when Rita and Hudson (apparently still vying for slots in the Olympics) bolted out and ran for the emergency-room door, leaving Sergeant Borsch to find legal parking on his own.

Once through the door, Rita and Hudson skidded to a halt.

It was as though William Rose Junior High School were conducting an assembly in the waiting room.

Only there was no presenter.

Just chaos.

"QUIET!" a voice across the room bellowed, and when Rita looked to see who had made the sound, she saw a bullish woman with bulging eyes. "WHERE'S THE LEGAL GUARDIAN FOR SAMANTHA KEYES?" Nurse Abbey shouted.

"Right here!" Rita called, holding up her hand.

The flash mob of teens turned to face her. And while they didn't break into a spontaneous rendition of Queen's "Bohemian Rhapsody," they were clearly in a Bohemian Rhapsody state of mind, parting to let this older woman through as they wondered, *Is this the real life? Is this just fantasy? . . .*

Then they watched the guardian and the nurse disappear behind the Swinging Door of (Maybe) Death.

3—NIGHT SHIFT

Waiting was hard. And although Hudson managed to slip through the swinging door to be with Rita, the rest were left to pace about. Or gnaw on nails. Or wring hands, or go into texting overdrive.

And as the wall clock ticked along from one agonizing minute to the next, sweeping past ten-thirty and on toward eleven, grumblings grew in the waiting room.

What was taking so long?

Why wasn't anyone coming out with an update?

Parents began showing up to fetch their children or sending messages demanding that they return home.

After all, it was a school night.

Final exams were looming.

And who was this Sammy Keyes person, anyway?

Which underscored why Marissa and Holly were so annoyed with the crowd. If these parents had never heard of Sammy Keyes (or were asking who "he" was), clearly their kids hadn't weathered the junior-high storm with Sammy. In fact, half of these kids had *been* the storm! What were they doing here?

It was a rhetorical question. Marissa and Holly knew what the mob was doing there. When the news about who Sammy's father was had broken a few months earlier, Sammy had instantly catapulted from scrappy girl to celebrity.

To (especially) Holly's delight, Sammy was still the scrappy girl she'd met at the soup kitchen over a year and a half ago and hadn't let her new "popular" status change her, holding tight to the friends who'd been there for her before the Big Discovery and keeping the others politely at bay.

But the tide of people trying to break into their circle was relentless and annoying—and now, as Holly and Marissa waited in agony for word about Sammy, very upsetting. To make matters worse, there seemed to be no sign of the tide going back *out* for the night. Once parents were brought up to speed about the celebrity connection, curfews were automatically extended, exam concerns brushed aside, and the question became: "Do you think *he'll* show up?"

"I wish they would all just *leave*," Holly whispered to Marissa as they both cast a resentful eye over the mob of teens and the growing number of parents.

"Except Billy and Casey," Marissa said. "They can stay."

"And Officer Borsch and his wife," Holly added (as Deb had appeared to comfort her uncharacteristically emotional husband).

"How about Heather?" Marissa asked.

"She's outta here!" Holly snarled, and after she and

Marissa shared a little fist bump, they continued scanning the crowd, whispering back and forth about who could stay and who should go.

And then *finally* Rita and Hudson emerged through the swinging door.

They looked pale.

Drained.

Like their hearts had forgotten how to circulate blood.

The waiting room fell quiet, and when the pallid seniors realized all eyes were on them and that *they* were expected to convey the news, Hudson gathered himself, cleared his throat, and said, "She's breathing on her own. There don't seem to be any broken bones, her heartbeat's regular and strong, but she hasn't regained consciousness. They're moving her over to ICU and will keep her there until she wakes up."

This news was received with great gusts of youthful relief.

She was going to be fine!

But amid the relief and jubilation, members of the over-sixteen set eyed each other cautiously.

Being unconscious for this long was a worry.

A big worry.

Better broken bones than an extended unconsciousness.

Better a ruptured spleen or a mangled meniscus or an impaled intestine (or even a grisly combination of all of them).

Doctors knew how to fix those things.

But unconsciousness? Maybe a coma? It was territory

that was frightening in its shadowy uncertainty. And as most adults knew, the longer the uncertainty, the more frightening it became.

Unconsciousness was, in reality, often just this side of death. Or on a path toward agonizing decisions involving ventilators and vegetative states and life-support systems.

But after a long moment of shadowy fear had crossed the adults' faces, there was a silent and almost unanimous shift toward a sunnier outlook as these same adults forced themselves to rally around optimism.

Maybe the poor girl's unconscious state was not just this side of death.

More likely, it was just *that* side of sleep!

It was simply her body's way of beginning the recovery process.

Besides, what purpose would it serve to sound the alarm or explain to the youngsters just how serious unconsciousness could be? Better to go home and get a good night's sleep. Better to focus on the positive and hope for the best. A child's innocence was short-lived enough these days.

So with murmurs among themselves and a few kind words to Rita and Hudson, the adults rounded up their teens (and whatever friends needed a ride), and slowly filtered out of the waiting room.

When the rest of their peers had left, Marissa and Holly (and a somewhat subdued Heather) joined Casey and Billy, and then went up to Rita and Hudson, who were quietly conferring with Meg. They still had questions. Big questions.

Like, How is she really?

Is she going to be all right?

When do they think she'll wake up?

But the only question either senior could even begin to answer was, What is ICU?

"Intensive-care unit," Hudson told them. "They'll monitor her round the clock."

"Can we see her?" Marissa asked, and her eyes were suddenly brimming with tears.

Hudson shook his head. "They wouldn't let *us* stay any longer. They say they'll call us when she wakes up."

Casey stepped forward. "But that's supposed to happen soon, right? She shouldn't wake up alone in a hospital!"

"We hope it happens soon," Hudson said cautiously. Then, in an effort to not walk further down that shadowy road, he volunteered some concrete and useful facts. "ICU is on the fourth floor of the main part of the hospital. Visiting hours are from eight a.m. to eight p.m." He forced some optimism into his voice. "Who should we call when we get some news?"

"Me!" the teens cried in unison, but in the end they agreed that since Marissa no longer had a cell phone, Casey would be the contact person.

At this point Gil Borsch came forward with Deb at his side. "Can I give you a lift?" he asked the seniors, then looked to the teens and added, "Do you need rides?" He focused on Marissa. "Not a good idea for you to go back to East Jasmine on your own this late at night."

"Oh," Marissa said. Then her cheeks flushed as she explained, "We don't live there anymore. We're . . . ," she looked away, "nearby now."

Gil Borsch studied her for a moment, but only for a moment. He'd heard rumors of gambling problems and a divorce, but gossip was for bottom-feeders, and he made a habit of trying to swim in cleaner waters. "Well, Deb or I can give any of you rides. We have two cars here, and your parents would probably like you home."

"I can help, too," Meg offered.

So rides were given and teens delivered, and seniors left to wearily climb the steps they'd flown from earlier. And back at their little cottage on Elm Street, Debra washed her face and went to bed, telling her husband (who was sitting in the living room in the dark), "Hon, do not stay up all night broodin'. You cannot help Sam by broodin'. All you'll be is tired tomorrow when she wakes up."

Words of wisdom, perhaps, but as the clock moved past midnight, Gil Borsch could still not shake the feeling that, regardless of how well she was monitored by the ICU staff, Sammy was alone.

And unprotected.

At last he moved his brooding from the living room to the shower (which he took in the dark), then tiptoed through the blackness of the bedroom to the closet, where he retrieved his uniform and regulation shoes. He dressed in the darkness of the kitchen, donned his personal holster and gun, and slipped out into the night.

On his way back to the hospital, he focused on getting his story straight, reminding himself that a serviceable lie was always close neighbors with the truth, and that a lie that *should* be the truth was barely a lie at all.

Then, knowing the hospital's main lobby doors were

25

locked after nine p.m., he went back to the ER entrance and gained access to the main section of the hospital without being questioned. He then rode an elevator up to the fourth floor, followed the signs to the ICU, and strode confidently through the waiting room area and up to the nurses' station. "I've been assigned watch on Samantha Keyes," he said as he flashed his ID at the nurse sitting behind the counter. "Attempted homicide victim. The perpetrator is still at large."

Perhaps it was that violent-crime victims often landed in the ICU, or perhaps it was the authority with which Sergeant Borsch presented himself (or maybe just that it was the night shift, where energy supplies were limited and making easy things hard was just not worth it), but the lawman's intentions were met with no resistance. The nurse simply checked her roster, pointed down the sterile corridor to her left, and said, "Room 411."

Rooms in the ICU were private, and 411 was located near the end of the hallway, on the right. Gil Borsch hesitated at its open doorway. A light was on inside, and the foot of Sammy's bed was visible past a drawn curtain.

In his many years on the force, Gil Borsch had seen his share of gruesome and tragic. If you joined the police force expecting to keep your cookies down, you learned in a hurry that you'd been one naïve chump. The first time an officer had to report to a scene where brains had been splattered against the wall, or a child had been hit by a car, or a decaying body had been discovered in a cellar . . . that was when the fantasy of the job instantly became the reality.

That was when every cop became a cookie chucker.

Including Officer Borsch.

So the lawman had experience. He knew that turning the corner past the curtain that shielded his view of Sammy and stepping through the barrier between imagination and reality was something he couldn't reverse after he'd done it.

There was no undo command for what would be hard-written into his memory.

Still. There was no turning back. No chickening out. No not facing what he really didn't want to face.

And so he stepped forward.

And then, there she was.

His first reaction was one of enormous relief.

Her face was fine!

There was a bruise and a scrape, but . . . he had imagined much worse. And although her arms were wrapped in gauze and her *head* was wrapped in gauze and there were tubes going into her and wires coming off of her, her face was fine!

Almost . . . angelic.

"Sammy," he whispered as he moved closer. "It's your buddy the Borschman." He grinned. "Yes, I know you call me that." He stared at her for a long minute before whispering, "Who *did* this to you?" A lump began forming in his throat as he choked out, "And *why*?" He took a moment to compose himself, then whispered, "Did you really go there because of some nightie-napper? Who cares who's stealing nighties! Was it worth *this*?"

The lump in the lawman's throat had grown, and it silenced him until he gave a snort and said, "Just like me to start with an interrogation, huh? What am I, an idiot? That's what you're thinkin', right? Can't I see you're not doin' so hot?" He studied her a little longer, then shook his head. "You should have seen the waiting room earlier. It was packed with kids. I can't handle a room of teenagers on a good day, you know that. And here I had to go and tolerate it on a day like this?" He forced a laugh. "Thanks a lot, Sammy."

He stared at her, lying there while the monitors blipped and machinery softly hummed. "You gotta wake up, you hear me? Just come to and give me a hard time."

The lump in his throat was now bigger and badder than ever, so he clammed up and backed away from the bed, nearly colliding with a male orderly.

"Excuse me!" the orderly said. He was wearing white on white, had narrow, black-rimmed glasses, and (to the Borschman's immediate and irrational annoyance) had shaggy brown hair.

"Do you know when a doctor will be by?" Sergeant Borsch asked, composing himself as quickly as he could.

"Soon, I'm sure," the orderly said, and after a quick inspection of the area, nodded a good night, and left the room.

Gil Borsch turned back to Sammy, but after a few more silent minutes willing her to wake up, he turned away and found himself gazing out the window.

At first, he looked upward. (Perhaps for divine intervention, but even under these circumstances probably not.)

Then he looked below, at the circular drive to the main

entrance. It was empty. No vehicles coming or going. No illegal park jobs. Nothing.

Then he looked out, across the town, where the lights of Santa Martina twinkled quietly.

Deceptively.

There were no sirens, no burning buildings, no alarms clanging. But out there, the lawman knew, swirling between the twinkling lights like toxic vapors, violence and deceit and unspeakable crimes were taking place.

Out there, someone who'd thrown a fourteen-year-old girl off three flights of stairs was roaming free.

Gil Borsch turned away from the window, turned away from his thoughts, turned back to Sammy. "Don't worry. We'll get whoever did this to you. That's a promise."

Then he sat in a chair next to Sammy's bed and hunkered down, unaware that in an unoccupied room across the hallway, the shaggy-haired orderly was hiding in the shadows, waiting impatiently for him to leave.

4—TRACING FOOTSTEPS

Fortunately, Gil Borsch did not leave Room 411. Instead, he fell asleep in his chair. It was a log-sawing slumber, too. One that could easily be heard in the darkened room across the hallway. One that conveyed a clear and exasperating signal.

Room 411 would be inaccessible for quite some time.

Now, I wish I could tell you that Sergeant Borsch was awakened from his log-sawing slumber by Sammy calling, "Hey, Borschhead! Wake up!" but that's not what happened. Instead, the lawman was rousted from his sleep by a nurse named Joanna who jabbed him in the arm and told him he might want to seek a physician's help for his condition. "Your snoring's been shaking the walls since I got on shift," she said as she checked Sammy's vitals. "If that didn't wake this girl, nothing might."

"What was that?" Sergeant Borsch asked, because Nurse Joanna had muttered the last part and the lawman was still fighting through the thick, sticky cobwebs of a nightmare in which he was strapped down on an operating table while a man in a ski mask held a scalpel over his heart.

"Nothing," Nurse Joanna replied, unwilling to repeat something she shouldn't have said in the first place.

But Gil Borsch was still transitioning from one nightmare to another and was having trouble picking up on obvious clues. "Did you say she might not wake up?"

The nurse fiddled with Sammy's IV bag. "Aren't you supposed to be posted *outside* the room?"

This did not answer the question, but it did bring the lawman's questioning to an immediate halt, as it reminded him that he was there under false pretenses. And regardless of how legitimate those false pretenses might *seem,* since there had been no official watch ordered for Sammy, not only would his deception get him booted from the ICU, it would put him in major hot water at the station.

"Sleeping on the job's nice work if you can get it," the nurse added, tossing him a scowl as she left the room.

Clearly, Nurse Joanna knew how to deflect and destroy. And although it was only 5:45 a.m., Gil Borsch's mood was, indeed, destroyed. (Not that he ever woke up chipper, but in addition to the bad dream and the bad news, his bad sleeping posture had given him a bad kink in the neck.)

He got up and hovered over Sammy. "Wake up, would ya?" he growled, and when there was no response, he reached in and nudged her. "Sammy! Sammy, wake up!"

He was answered only by the silent blipping of her heart monitor. And the more he stood there, watching, the more the peaceful look on Sammy's face tortured him. What was with that angelic look? Where was the little hellion he'd grown to love?

Perhaps it was a form of emotional survival (or maybe just the call of addiction), but after he'd spent another minute searching Sammy's face for answers, his thoughts turned to coffee. He could feel a headache creeping up on him from behind, and experience had taught him that he needed to take it out before it had a chance to get a stronghold. (Or, in this case, join forces with the kink in his neck, which he also knew from years of experience was a wickedly crippling combination.)

So he needed coffee.

Now.

Unfortunately, he was faced with the complications of his lie. During a *legitimate* police watch placed on a patient, the attending officer couldn't just leave his post. One officer would relieve another, round the clock, until the watch was lifted.

But he needed coffee.

Now.

Asking at the nurses' station seemed like a dead end. Besides, there was the whole shaking-the-walls thing, and Gil Borsch did have a certain level of pride. He did not want to be the butt of jokes at the nurses' station, but since he most likely already was, he didn't want his face associated with those jokes.

Still.

He needed coffee.

Now!

Thinking through his options, he realized he did have a couple of things going in his favor: First, since he'd conducted his "watch" from inside the hospital room, there was the distinct possibility that his absence would go (by and large) unnoticed. And second, just a few yards away at the end of the hall was a door marked EXIT that (according to the door's graphic) accessed a stairwell.

Together these conditions would provide a surreptitious departure if he could manage to get to the exit door without being seen.

Now, it did cross his mind that he was a cop.

One who prided himself in walking the straight and narrow.

At designated intersections.

Between the white lines.

(Which is why jaywalkers sent him into such a tizzy.)

So casting an eye down the corridor to his left as a *deceptive* strategy caused a definite pang to shoot through Gil Borsch's law-abiding conscience (and another one to shoot through his kinked-up neck). But to his relief, the coast was clear, and with a quick hike of his pants and as much casual confidence as he could muster, he set out toward the exit on his right.

Moments later, he was safely through the door, but as he began hurrying down the steps, a disturbing thought shot through his law-abiding mind:

He was pulling a Sammy Keyes!

Sammy had done this exact move (only without the security of an enclosed stairwell) to get in and out of the Senior Highrise every day—even several times a day—for *years*. After he'd begun to suspect that she was living at the Highrise illegally, he'd staked it out, watching with binoculars (and a full thermos of coffee) from his parked car.

It had taken weeks, but he'd finally spotted her one morning as she'd slipped through the fifth-floor door and swept down the fire escape like an ethereal cat floating through shadows.

"I knew it! I knew it!" he'd cried, validated at last.

And now here he was, doing the same thing. (Only, he noted ruefully as he clomped along, there was nothing remotely catlike about him.)

Now, having been to the hospital many times on police business, Gil Borsch knew how to find the cafeteria.

First floor, west wing.

So when he reached the bottom of the stairs, he did not take the exit door to his left, which would have led him outside the building. Rather, he pushed through the door straight ahead, which left him within easy striking distance of the cafeteria.

What he did *not* know—and what caused an audible growl to emerge from the depths of his deprived gut—was the cafeteria's hours of operation.

6:30 a.m.–8:00 p.m.

But outside the closed grating he discovered (to his enormous relief) a vending machine where coffee could be purchased. So after swiping a card and pushing the appropriate buttons he emerged victorious with a coffee-colored cardboard cup. And although the concoction inside it was barely warm (and oddly pasty), at least it was caffeinated.

On his fourth gulp, his phone rang.

"Borsch here," he said with uncharacteristic eagerness.

But it was not news about Sammy.

It was his wife, wondering where in the world he was.

So the lawman fessed up, telling her not only where he was, but where he'd been, and where he was going. And after a weary conversation convincing Deb that he was doing what he was doing because it was the only thing *to* do, and that if you wanted a job done right you had to do it yourself, and that this job—*especially* this job—was one that *had* to be done right, he told her he loved her and would see her later. Then he gulped down the rest of his coffee and walked out of the hospital, focused on a new mission.

Now, perhaps it was simply because nature abhors a vacuum, or perhaps it was a bit of cosmic good luck, or maybe it was simply that Sammy's friends and family were really worried about her and willing to break rules and curfews and common sense to visit her, but that chair in Room 411 didn't stay vacant for very long.

Billy Pratt hadn't slept a wink all night and had finally given up trying. He was usually on his way to school before either of his parents was up anyway, so it was easy for him to slip out the front door and hoof it over to the hospital.

To his surprise, the hospital's main lobby door was locked. And, afraid of being turned back if he followed the instructions on the placard directing people to the ER, he began looking for other entrances.

Something he told himself Sammy might do.

As he made his way along the building's periphery, he came upon several doors.

All unmarked.

All locked.

And as he turned yet another corner and found himself

alone on what appeared to be a dead-end route in the still-shadowy light of early morning, fear began tiptoeing along beside him.

What was he doing?

He tried shaking it off.

Who would be lurking around the side of a hospital?

And for what?

He saw another door not far away, so he hurried toward it. But as he approached, fear held on like a cape, pulling at his shoulders, covering him with warning.

Turn around!

Which is exactly what he would have done after that one final door had it not been for one little detail.

The door opened!

And led to a stairwell!

Silly Billy, he told himself. What was there to be afraid of?

Not knowing where he was going (but believing he was at least making progress), he hurried up the stairs, trying the interior doors at each level until he finally found one unlocked on the fourth floor.

And then, in what seemed to Billy to be a miracle (or maybe an omen, or, at least, a stroke of astounding good luck), he found Sammy inside Room 411.

"Sammy-keyesta!" he whispered, looking at his gauze-wrapped, tube-strapped friend. And then the boy who always had something to say just stood there, without words.

"You need to leave," a voice behind him said.

Billy turned around and saw a man in green scrubs. And on an ordinary day and under ordinary circumstances,

Billy Pratt might have put up a little resistance before complying with the request. But this wasn't some ordinary day and these weren't ordinary circumstances, so instead what came from the mouth of Billy Pratt was, "I'm not leaving."

"Yes, you are. You need to leave *now*," the orderly said.

But it was a weird, hissy command that came through the teeth.

Which seemed . . . odd to Billy. And made him tune in to other things about the orderly. Things like his scruffy hair. And that behind the boxy glasses, there were dark circles under the man's eyes. And, wow, the cheek stubbles. There were cheek stubbles for miles!

He wasn't going to let some scruffy dude with baggy eyes and a hissy voice tell him what to do!

"I'm stayin'," Billy said. "And you need to get shavin'."

The orderly stared at him, then felt his cheek.

"You been up all night, or what?" Billy asked. Then he sat down in the chair where Gil Borsch had been and watched (somewhat stupefied) as his defiance (for once) had its desired effect and the orderly turned without another hissy word and left the room.

After leaving the hospital, Sergeant Borsch had gone directly to the police station, where he had learned (to his frustration) that there were no leads in the Keyes case. Then, after brooding through the dayshift briefing, he convinced his superiors to let him take over the investigation and drove a squad car to the Senior Highrise.

He did not go inside the lobby.

Instead, he retraced the steps Holly had described

Sammy taking, walking along the sidewalk, ducking behind a tall hedge, making his way past an alcove where the trash chute emptied into a Dumpster, toward the fire escape.

As he neared the steps, his heart began to pound and sweat began to pour from him, but he really couldn't understand why. It was daylight and still cool out. He was armed and in no obvious danger. Yet his heart hadn't pounded this way since . . . well, since the Psycho Kitty Incident where he'd been duct-taped and thrown in the back of a van, certain (for hours) that he would be murdered (any minute) and dumped on the side of the road.

In an effort to calm himself, Sergeant Borsch took several deep breaths, then began scouring the scene—the grounds, the bushes, and finally the steps. It bothered him that there was no yellow crime-scene tape cordoning off the area. Who had determined there was no evidence to be gathered? It had been dark when the crime was committed, and it had only been daylight now for about two hours.

What was wrong with his department?

Didn't they understand how important this was?

It also bothered him that the area looked as though nothing had happened. Even the bushes appeared to be unscathed, seemingly denying that a girl had crash-landed into them.

Finally, he began up the fire escape, slowly and meticulously inspecting each level and trying each door to see if entry was possible.

He found nothing. And at each level the door was latched and locked until the fifth floor, where the door was just as Sammy had rigged it—locked, but not latched.

With the sigh of a man caught between justice and heartache, Gil Borsch took a last look around, then went inside.

The Highrise wasn't a typical tenement building where residents scurried to their corners like guilty rats when a man with a badge appeared. The tenants in this apartment complex were more like mice—nosy and twitchy, curious but wary.

And although the hallway was quiet, with all the doors closed tight, that changed after Sergeant Borsch knocked at Sammy's grandmother's old apartment.

"She moved," a voice behind him said, and when he turned toward the sound, he saw a slice of a pale, wrinkled face peering at him through a barely opened door.

The lawman already knew that Rita had moved, so he couldn't really say why he'd knocked. Perhaps he was longing to go back in time—longing for Rita to open the door and pretend Sammy wasn't there, when in fact she was hiding in the closet.

"No new tenant?" Sergeant Borsch asked.

The wrinkles moved side to side. "Supposedly this week."

"And supposedly a *man*," another female voice said through a door that had inched open across the way.

The first door opened an itty-bit more. "That's been the rumor for a month."

"But Violet's moved into Rose's place," a third woman volunteered.

"Anyone remember Daisy?" squeaked a fourth voice, from yet another barely opened door.

"Oh, she was a piece of work," the first voice said.

"*She* was?" the third voice said, and her door opened a crack farther, too. "Rita's the one I always thought was hiding something."

"Yeah," came the second voice. "And look—cops are *still* knockin'."

Perhaps it was the aches and pains of age that had these women up early. Or maybe they'd just fallen asleep in front of their televisions at six-thirty the night before and were full up on sleep and looking for some excitement. (Or, at least, gossip.) Regardless, it was not yet eight a.m. and Sergeant Borsch was already in the thick of it, surrounded by twitching noses and squeaking voices. Under normal circumstances he would have insisted that the associated faces and bodies show themselves, but he suspected he was probably better off with this limited view of things. So he simply asked, "Did any of you hear or see someone come down this hallway last night?"

His question was met with twitchy silence.

"It would have been sometime after nine o'clock," he added.

The twitchy silence continued until the wrinkles behind Door #1 finally said, "I was asleep," which brought a chorus of similar comments from the others, and a bonus remark from Door #3: "Haven't seen nine o'clock since they removed my gall bladder."

And after another minute of conversation that went nowhere, the voices came together in one final piece of advice: "Go see Mr. Garnucci."

Gil Borsch was not a fan of Vince Garnucci. Garnucci

was the building's manager, and although he did seem to know all the residents, he shouted when he spoke, he injected off-topic stories about his wacky grandmother, and he was skinny.

Gil Borsch wasn't comfortable around skinny.

But he had a job to do, and that trumped any annoyance he might feel over a loud, skinny fella whose ninety-five-year-old grandmother still rode a bicycle.

So after inspecting both the stairway and the elevator for clues (and determining that, like the exterior of the building, the interior didn't offer a single surface from which he'd be able to lift fingerprints), he found himself in the lobby.

"Officer Borsch!" the manager shouted from behind his desk.

The greeting was clearly meant to convey warmth and welcome, but the lawman noted the underlying nervousness that always seemed present when he dealt with Vince Garnucci.

Part of that whole skinny thing.

Plus, Gil Borsch was no longer an officer. His promotion to sergeant had been over a year ago, and Vince Garnucci knew it.

The lawman let it slide. "Morning, Garnucci. I understand you gave a report on the events of last night, but I'm just following up."

"Sure, sure," the manager said, and then proceeded to spend the next five minutes talking his way down a long, winding road to nowhere.

"So to sum up," Sergeant Borsch finally said, "nobody

came through the lobby, you heard nothing either inside or outside, and none of the residents reported anything."

"That sums it up, yeah," Mr. Garnucci said, then cocked his head a little and asked, "Has the victim died? And what were they doing on the fire escape?"

Sergeant Borsch sucked on a tooth for a moment, debating whether to break the news of the victim's identity. He knew the manager was fond of Sammy, but she was a minor and there were rules. Laws, even. Besides, something about the man's demeanor was . . . troubling.

Instead, he simply said, "We don't know."

"But . . . wait . . . how did you get inside the building?"

"I used the back entrance," the lawman said, surprised by how easily the lie had slipped off his tongue.

"It's unlocked?"

Sergeant Borsch moved toward the front door. "Have a good day, Garnucci." And before the manager could protest, he was gone.

5—PRAYERS

So where were Sammy's mother and father in all of this?

Rita did try to reach Lana while she was waiting at the ER, but couldn't connect to her daughter in person and couldn't bring herself to leave a message that said more than "Call me as soon as you can."

Which Lana, being Lana, didn't.

So after Rita and Hudson returned to their Cypress Street home around midnight, Rita steadied herself and tried once again to reach her daughter.

This time, Lana answered.

There's a certain level of disbelief that occurs when a person's hit with bad news. Questions like Are you sure? Is she okay? What happened? shoot from the mouth.

Unless, of course, you're Lana Keyes. Then your disbelief comes out this way:

"Are you a tabloid reporter trying to get a reaction out of me?"

And if you're *Rita* Keyes and your daughter's pulled one too many diva reversals on you (where somehow the drama became all about her), and you're exhausted from hours at the hospital and feel the weight of the world on your shoulders, what might (and very well *should*) shoot from your mouth is, "No, you self-absorbed ditz. This is your mother and you need to get here *now*."

But that's not what Rita said.

As you probably already know, Rita Keyes is a class act. And although her trigger finger was twitching, she managed to keep her fully loaded arsenal of retorts holstered. "Lana," she said wearily. "I am not a tabloid reporter. I am your mother."

"Prove it."

Rita's tired eyebrow perked to life.

Lana had asked for it.

So Rita shot straight to the heart. "You were born in the year—"

"Stop! Fine! Okay!" Lana sputtered, clearly worried that some tabloid reporter might be listening in. But with the legitimacy of the call resolved, the urgency behind it seemed to finally sink in. "Now, what happened to Samantha?"

Rita was through trying to break the news gently. "She fell three floors off the side of the Highrise. Fortunately, she landed in a thick hedge."

"So . . . is she all right?"

"We don't know."

"You don't know? What do you mean you don't know? How can you not know?" And then with a sudden gasp she asked, "Was there *blood*?"

The pitch of Lana's voice had risen considerably, and since blood was one of those faint-inducing triggers that seemed to plague the actress, Rita did not fire off with,

"She fell three floors! What do you *think*?" She instead struggled to remain calm and stick to the big picture: Sammy was in the hospital, unconscious. Lana needed to get to Santa Martina right away.

And Darren needed to be told.

"Do you want me to call him?" Rita asked, and in some ways she dreaded the thought of breaking the news to Samantha's father more than breaking it to her own daughter. Darren had only known Sammy (or that he even *had* a daughter) for a few months, but in that time she had become the sunshine of his life, the high harmony of a song that now played in his heart.

Witnessing this had brought great joy to Rita. Especially since it seemed that, for Lana, Sammy had been more like the stormy cloud *covering* the sunshine, the dissonant chord in the movie score that crescendoed through the life she had always imagined for herself.

A life that she was, ironically, finally realizing now that she'd told the truth and reunited with Sammy's father.

"Lana?" Rita asked, because her question had been met with silence.

"He's in the middle of a show," Lana replied. "It'll be two or three a.m. before I can reach him."

"Is he in Las Vegas?" Rita asked.

"No, he's here in LA. Is Samantha at Community?"

"Yes. In ICU."

"In ICU?!" Lana gasped.

To which Rita could easily have snapped, "She fell three floors! Be glad she's not at the morgue!" but she didn't. She instead gave Lana the hospital's number and visiting hours and told her to get to town as soon as possible, then went to bed.

She could not, however, fall asleep. So when the phone rang an hour later, she snatched it up right away, praying it was good news about her granddaughter. "Yes?"

But it wasn't news about Sammy. It was Lana, and she was in full diva mode. "I can't get information out of anybody!" she cried (without so much as a hello or an I'm-sorry-if-I-woke-you). "All I can get out of the hospital is that she's stable!"

"Has she woken up?"

"No!"

Hudson was wide awake now, too, and asked Rita, "Is that the doctor? Has she woken up?"

Rita's rapid head wobbling and verbal reply into the phone answered both his questions simultaneously. "But stable is a positive thing, Lana. Calm down."

"Calm down?" Lana cried. "Calm down? I can't get through to anybody! Marissa's number is disconnected—"

"They've moved, Lana."

"Nobody told me that! And that police officer? The one Samantha was a bridesmaid for? His first name's Gilbert, right?"

"That's right."

"Well, he's not listed—"

"He's a police officer, Lana. Of course he's not listed."

"Well, I couldn't find a number for Casey, either! And I sure wasn't calling Warren or Candi! So I tried the Doggy Den, but it's not listed, either! It's a business! Why isn't it listed?"

"Because it's the Pup Parlor, not the Doggy Den, Lana. And what good would that have done you? No business would answer the phone at this hour!"

"But her friend who saw what happened lives there!"

"She lives in the apartment *above* the Pup Parlor, Lana. It's a separate number."

"WHY DON'T I HAVE ANYBODY'S NUMBER?"

After it was safe to put the phone back to her ear, Rita did so and said, "I think that's a question you might want to ask yourself," and hung up with a *hrmph*.

Of course the phone rang again five seconds later, but this time Hudson picked up, giving his wife a gentle "Let me."

And Hudson, being Hudson, managed to defuse the situation and help Lana focus on what *could* be done (like packing and making travel plans) instead of what served no purpose (like calling people in the middle of the night). He also promised her she'd be the first person they'd call if they got news about Sammy, and asked her to do likewise. "We'll meet you at the hospital," he told her. And after a small hesitation during which he tried to balance the reality of the situation with the needs of a desperate mother, he added, "She's got a strong spirit, Lana. We all just have to pray that she pulls through this."

Once off the phone, Hudson assured his wife that Lana and Darren would arrive as soon as possible and that the best thing they could do for Sammy was to get some rest so they wouldn't be too exhausted to be useful when Sammy awoke. Then he went to the kitchen, rummaged through the herbal teas Rita had moved in with her, and selected chamomile (as the box boasted calming properties and showed a cozy bear in a nightcap).

Unfortunately, the brew had no effect on either Rita or Hudson, and by five-thirty, both had given up on sleep and were on their way to St. Mary's Church.

Having never gone to pray at this early hour before, the couple were a little surprised to find the door to the main church unlocked. Inside, there were a few candles burning at the altar, but the lights were off and the large room was ominously still.

Rita whispered, "Let's just go to the side chapel," but then through the darkness came the *ticky-tack*ing of toenails on tile.

Hudson let out a soft whistle and whispered, "Gregory! Here, boy!" Soon a Welsh terrier appeared from between the pews. "Where's your master, huh?" Hudson asked as the dog approached.

"Why, good mornin'," came a voice that instantly conjured up visions of rolling green hills and four-leaf clovers. "What brings you two here at this hour?"

"Father Mayhew!" Rita cried, and suddenly she was in tears. "Oh, please. Pray with us."

"My dear, what is wrong?" the priest asked, hurrying over (while Gregory took the opportunity to fetch his favorite chew—a carrot).

And so it came out. About Sammy and the fall and the stranger on the stairs and her condition in the hospital.

Father Mayhew had had his own escapades with Sammy and knew her to be the sort of girl you wished were your own (well, if you weren't a priest, and you didn't mind all the trouble that seemed to follow her). So he got on his knees beside Rita and Hudson and prayed with an earnest heart (and a lilting Irish brogue), begging God for mercy and compassion and reason.

And Gregory, who seemed to understand that this was serious, did not press the slobbery carrot he'd retrieved on Hudson in an effort to get him to play fetch, but rather sat quietly with his paws touching, as if doing what he could to help get the word up to God.

When they'd all murmured "Amen" (and Gregory was free to focus again on the wonders of his carrot), Rita and Hudson gave Father Mayhew their sincere thanks and the priest, in turn, assured them that he would "continue to pray for young Samantha."

Then the seniors stepped out into the cool dawn air and drove toward the hospital, unaware that Sergeant Borsch had kept a night watch or that Billy Pratt had snuck into Room 411.

It was a new day.

A new shift would soon begin in the ICU.

And the hospital staff were about to realize that, although they'd attended to everyone from gang lords to the governor, they'd never experienced anyone like Samantha Josephine Keyes.

Even in a coma, the girl was trouble.

6—DITCHERS

Before it flared up again at Community Hospital, trouble sparked to life at William Rose Junior High School. It began with concern—with Holly and Marissa and their good friend Dot DeVries worrying aloud among other classmates.

It ended with students ditching school.

After all, who cared about mathematics or history or the rules of constructing a multi-paragraph essay? When a life hung in the balance, it was hard to fathom how mastering negative exponents or understanding the framework of an agrarian society or even how to write a general statement of commentary could possibly matter. (It was hard to fathom regardless!)

It didn't seem important to these students that the life in question belonged to someone most of them didn't really know. Or someone they'd spent most of seventh grade (and a good stretch of eighth) ridiculing.

Or whispering about.

(Or, at least, tolerating the whispers about.)

It was still . . . upsetting.

Sammy was one of *them*. And she'd been thrown seven

floors (according to the growing rumors) to her near (and impending) death! It was unreasonable for anyone to expect them to concentrate on schoolwork at a time like this! They needed to support their classmate!

So by midmorning an exodus had begun. And as texts flew and word got around, the vacant seats grew in number until some classrooms were so woefully empty that by lunchtime teachers began questioning the use of being at school themselves.

Now, many of these students (ditchers though they were) *did* go to the hospital. But the reality of being inside even the main lobby of an institution for the injured and infirm freaked them out. Tears welled. Friends hugged. Whispers swirled.

And then they got the heck out of there.

And regrouped at the mall.

In the food court.

Where fries were cheap and Pepsi refills were free.

Marissa, Holly, and Dot were not the first ones to reach the hospital (because Dot had never ditched and it took some real convincing). So the senior volunteers sitting behind the reception desk had already seen a revolving cast of teens and had a good idea what these three girls wanted.

"Here about Samantha Keyes?" one of the volunteers asked.

"Yes, ma'am," Holly replied.

"Are you actually staying?" the volunteer pressed. "Because if you're not, save me the name badges, would you? I'm getting tired of throwing them away."

When you're a volunteer, you can get away with being

a little snippy (especially to teenagers). But after the girls assured her that they were indeed staying, the volunteer lightened up a little and instructed them to sign in, then issued those valuable badges (which were nothing more than your basic Avery #8395 label with VISITOR printed in blue across the top). "The elevator's down that way," she said, motioning to her left. "Go up to the fourth floor, follow the signs to ICU. She's in Room 411."

For anyone who has not done it before, moving beyond the reception desk of Santa Martina's Community Hospital is like stepping over a threshold into a different realm. The paint scheme changes from warm, earthen tones to a pale (or—let's just say it, shall we—*ghastly*) green. The flooring switches from carpeting to a hard, epoxied surface (probably cement), and instead of large, bold murals of local landscapes, Sani-Foam dispensers adorn the walls.

The smell also changes.

As do the sounds.

"It's so quiet," Marissa whispered as they waited for the elevator. "And . . . sterile."

Holly whispered, "Well, you want a hospital to be sterile, right?"

"Maybe we should have brought something?" Dot said. "Like flowers? Or balloons?"

Marissa gasped. "We should go back and get something!"

But just then the wide steel elevator door opened, and the cool, gaping hole it exposed seemed to suck them forward. Any thoughts of flowers and balloons were abandoned in the hallway.

"Even the elevator's creepy," Marissa whispered after Holly had pressed the 4 button.

Holly nodded. "Big enough for a gurney."

Dot's eyes darted around. "Do you think Sammy was brought up in here?"

It was a thought that sent shivers down the three girls' spines, and all three were glad to step out of the giant steel box and into a fourth-floor hallway, where there was (at first) only one direction to go:

Left.

Then (after navigating a maze of corridors and asking directions twice) the girls turned a corner (to the left) and discovered they were not the first ones of their friends to arrive in the ICU waiting room—a quiet area between open corridors and a nurses' station.

"Billy!" Marissa whispered (as whispering still seemed to be the proper mode of communication). "Is there any news? How long have you been here?"

Billy's eyes were rimmed in red, and his face looked pale. It was as though all the blood that normally ran through his cheeks had been diverted to his eyes. "No change," he said bleakly. "Casey's in with her now."

A surge of jealousy rushed through Marissa. She tried to stem it, telling herself that she was being ridiculous, but she couldn't entirely stop it. Casey had only been in the picture for about a year. *She'd* been Sammy's best friend since the third grade. *She* should have been the friend to see her first.

And then things got worse.

After talking to Billy for a bit (and learning that Lana

and Darren had been there earlier with Rita and Hudson), Marissa noticed two people walking toward them from down the ICU corridor.

Casey was one of them.

Heather was the other.

"You've got to be kidding me!" Marissa cried (and it was not, I assure you, a whisper).

"Down, girl," Billy warned her.

But Holly was shaking her head in complete solidarity with Marissa. "That is so not right," she whispered.

"Check your weapons," Billy said. "This is not about you or Heather or your stupid war. This is about Sammy."

Which, Marissa knew, was right.

But still.

It was so wrong!

"How is she?" Billy asked when Casey and Heather were upon them.

Casey couldn't seem to make eye contact with anything but the floor. "The same," he said, his voice hoarse and tired.

And then, to everyone's surprise, Heather threw herself into Marissa's arms and sobbed, "It's horrible! There are tubes and monitors everywhere, and she's just *lying* there!"

As Heather sobbed, her globby mascara ran and her foundation smeared, and Marissa's shirt (which was a lovely pastel yellow) became smudged and splotched and (thanks to Heather's runny nose) snotty and, well, *disgusting*.

Compounding the undeniable grossness of the hug was the weirdness of it. Marissa tried to remember if she'd ever so much as touched Heather. *Sammy* certainly had (usually with a fist). But even in softball Marissa couldn't remember having had any sort of physical contact with the wild redhead.

And certainly not a hug!

Plus, Heather only turned on the spigots in front of males. Friends, teachers, parents . . . anyone on whom the ol' tear routine worked.

Which pretty much excluded the female students at William Rose, and it certainly excluded her!

So Marissa was dumbstruck. And (although awkward and gross) the hug threw her enough that before she could shove the snotty redhead off of her with a "What are you *doing*?" Heather sniffed and pulled back on her own. "She looks awful!" she wailed. "Just awful!"

Casey stepped in with a sharp "Heather!" then turned to Marissa. "Sammy looks like she's sleeping, that's all."

"With tubes and wires and bandages everywhere!" Heather cried.

"Quit it!" Casey snapped.

With a huff, Marissa grabbed Holly and Dot and said, "We're going to go see for ourselves."

"Better wait a few minutes," Casey said. "They kicked us out so they could . . . do stuff."

"And it's only two visitors at a time," Billy called.

Marissa might have pressed on regardless, just to get away from Heather, but a nurse was heading their way. A nurse who was wearing a smock with a colorful pattern of guitars. Blue ones, green ones, yellow ones, red ones . . . it was a cheerful assemblage of six-strings, and it made for a pleasant pre-introduction.

As did her name badge, which said FAITH.

But then came the actual introduction.

Or, rather, request for information.

"Are y'all related to Samantha Keyes?" the nurse asked.

"We're . . . friends," Marissa said.

"But . . . you can probably verify . . . the man that was here before . . . her dad . . ."

The assemblage of six teens stared at her, not believing (and yet absolutely knowing) what was about to come out of her mouth.

". . . is he really *the* Darren Cole?"

For the others, a protective shield of lies (or strategic non-answers) began to form, but Heather (in a strange and ironic twist) told the truth. "Yes, he is."

It would take less than an hour for it to become clear that it would have been better—much, much better—to lie.

7—VISITORS

Lana Keyes and Darren Cole had arrived together at Community Hospital shortly after Rita and Hudson had been allowed to enter Sammy's room (where they had displaced a solemn Billy Pratt, who had convinced a day-shift nurse that a night-shift nurse had taken mercy on his poor pummeled heart and let him stay).

And later, after a nurse (with panting puppies on her smock) had come in to enforce the two-person rule, Rita and Hudson had graciously exited, telling Lana and Darren to meet them down in the hospital cafeteria when they were done.

With Hudson's reasoned influence over Lana gone, what occurred next was the stuff of which soap operas are made. Demands. Tantrums. Tears. Threats. Cajolery.

Your basic diva-driven drama.

And while Lana whipped the ICU staff into a soapy froth, Darren struggled with the nauseating sense that he'd already been robbed of the first fourteen years of Sammy's life and couldn't bear the thought of being robbed of the rest. He'd made peace in his mind (and with Lana) over what had happened, but that was because he had the future to look forward to. The next fourteen years and beyond, where he would make up for lost time.

But if that time was now gone?

If he'd been robbed twice?

There was no peace to be found in that scenario.

Plus, he was wrestling with the unshakable notion that he was somehow responsible for what had happened to Sammy. He should have been there. He should have taken charge of the living arrangements. He should have done something, anything, to keep her safe.

There was also the powerful urge to get the guy who'd done this. To drag him up three flights and hurl him overboard.

No bushes required.

Or desired.

So inside Darren, anger, regret, revenge, and remorse rang loudly, but like phase-canceling waveforms of emotion, the result was silence.

The silence of disbelief.

And after the doctor (a physician by the name of Dr. Jha) had at last been consulted, the recommended course of action was still the same:

Wait and see.

With this new non-news, Darren corralled his emotions and took to his phone, searching the internet, contacting friends, finding specialists, pulling every string he could grasp, looking for something, anything, that might help.

Lana, meanwhile, sobbed at Sammy's bedside, working herself into a positive frenzy of questions and indictments. "Oh, darling," she gasped, between sobs. "How in the world could this have happened? Why did you go back to that awful place? Who did this to you?" And then, after another makeup-messing bout with tears, "I just don't understand why life has to be so horrible and hard and cruel! Samantha, please. *Please*, wake up!"

Overcome with emotion (and a conflicting desire to not become puffy-eyed), Lana sequestered herself in the bathroom, where cool water and a mirror were at her disposal.

Which left Darren alone with his daughter.

"Hey, kiddo," he said, slipping his hand over Sammy's. "It's your dad. Can you hear me?"

And then he just stood there with a rock (and no roll) in his throat.

He wanted to tell her that everything was going to be okay and that he was on top of tracking down a specialist. He wanted to sound optimistic and assured and strong. Like a dad was supposed to be.

But what he really felt was scared.

More scared than he'd ever been.

So again, he was silent.

And he was just standing there, silently holding her hand, when an orderly swept in. "Oh, sorry," the orderly murmured, gazing through long black bangs. "I'll come back." And before Darren could collect himself to ask questions or encourage him to go about his business, the orderly made a graceful exit, leaving the rocker alone with his fears (and his daughter, of course).

Then Lana came out of the bathroom with her dark glasses on, and after another few minutes of hovering around Sammy's bed, she and Darren left the room and were almost immediately replaced by Casey and Heather.

So by the time Marissa, Holly, and Dot appeared on the scene, there had already been a steady stream of anxious (as well as unauthorized) visitors, and the ICU staff seemed to have lost its will to resist. Not only was it (for once) a slow day in the ICU, but the staff's preoccupation with an internet search on Darren Cole resulted in a definite relaxing of the rules, which became evident when (despite Billy's citing of the two-visitor rule) nobody interfered as Marissa, Holly, and Dot all entered the corridor that led to Room 411.

Not being a rule breaker, Dot was aflutter with nerves as they moved down the corridor, but Marissa managed to steel herself and channel Sammy, saying, "Just act cool."

Holly, of course, was already familiar with this concept, having regularly broken many rules (not to mention laws) during her young life. So, between the two of them, the three of them made it down to Sammy's room without incident.

"Look at her," Marissa whispered when they'd surrounded the bed. "She looks so . . ."

"Peaceful?" Dot whispered.

Marissa nodded. "Yes."

"I've heard you're supposed to talk to people who are in comas," Holly whispered from the foot of the bed.

Dot nodded. "And stimulate them."

"Stimulate them?" Marissa asked.

"Like touch them?"

Dot (being a gentle soul) reached out and stroked

Sammy's leg through the bedding. But Holly (whose soul harbored painful splinters and cracks) did not have deep reserves of patience and went straight for the toes.

"What are you *doing*?" Marissa whispered, because Holly had dug beneath the covers and was wiggling and tickling and pinching.

"Wiggling and tickling and pinching," Holly replied.

Unfortunately, the only one this activity seemed to stimulate was Marissa. "Stop it!" she cried. "How would *you* like someone wiggling and tickling and pinching *you* when you couldn't do anything about it?"

"Maybe I'd wake up and slap 'em!" Holly snapped.

But she did stop.

And then she burst into tears.

"Oh, Holly," Dot said, scooping an arm around her. Then she looked at Marissa and mouthed, "We'll meet you outside," and eased Holly out of the room.

Which left Marissa alone with her best friend.

"Sammy," Marissa said, pulling up a chair beside the bed after she'd stared at her friend awhile. "You need to wake up, okay? You need to wake up and take your finals and finish junior high and start high school and live your life!" She frowned, then added, "Okay, so the thought of finals would make *me* want to stay asleep, too, but you know what I'm saying!" And then, feeling like the words were coming out all wrong, Marissa started babbling. "Look, you have to wake up. Everything is finally going great for you! You've got an awesome boyfriend, you've got an awesome *dad*, you're out of the Highrise, and Heather's not lurking around trying to sabotage you anymore!" She frowned again. "That doesn't mean I *like* her or *trust* her, but at least things are better than they were before. . . ."

Feeling off track again, Marissa shook her head and said, "Never mind about Heather. Worry about *me*, would you? I don't know what I'd do without you!" She went quiet for a minute, then sighed and said, "Remember last year when I got caught at the top of that stupid chain-link fence behind the Heavenly Hotel? I was stuck and petrified, and you came up and unhooked my pants and helped me down. My *life* has been like that. I wind up somewhere, stuck and scared, and you always seem to know how to help me down. Like with Danny? I was *so* stuck and helpless and stupid, but you helped me get over him."

And although Sammy would almost certainly have loved the comparison between Marissa's relationship with Danny Urbanski and being stuck on the detached and decrepit chain-link fence behind the seedy Heavenly Hotel, she gave no indication of this.

She just lay there, silent.

And as Sammy lay there, silent, Marissa thought. And remembered. And then she began to fill that silence. "Actually, the fence was nothing compared to going into the Bush House. . . . Do you remember that? And finding Chauncy LeBard all tied up with a monster mask on? Was that scary, or what?" She thought some more. "And that time in Sisquane? When we went looking for a missing *pig* and wound up battling it out with a drug dealer?" She shook her head. "I thought for sure we were going to die! But at least *he* was the one trapped in the cellar that time, which was way better than the time *we* were trapped in a basement by that gang guy! Remember that? With all those creepy black widow spiders?!" She shivered. "I *knew* we were gonna die that time. I still have nightmares about being trapped down there."

At this point Marissa realized that if Sammy *could* hear her, she might well be giving *her* nightmares. So she steered away from memories of deadly gang leaders and drove the conversation toward a brighter destination:

Hollywood.

"What about that time we snuck away to visit your mother? Remember how we threw that mattress out of the window so we could jump on it to escape that crazy mummy lady? And how that guy Max . . ."

But suddenly Marissa realized that she was heading off a cliff with that misadventure, too—that their unauthorized trip to Hollywood had also involved a very creepy ending.

So Marissa swerved in another direction.

"How about that time we went ice blocking after the Farewell Dance and Billy had those chicken bones and was acting like a pirate going 'Aaargh,' and then—" She came to a screeching halt. "Shoot! That one turned out all scary and gruesome, too!" She stared at her friend and shook her head. "It was even worse than finding those two skulls in the graveyard on Halloween." She shivered again. "And that turned out to be organized crime! Organized crime, Sammy! How do we get ourselves into these things?"

And then, as she took a deep breath to calm herself, a voice behind her said, "We need to make a list."

Marissa spun around.

Heather Acosta was standing right there.

"How long have you been spying on us?" Marissa demanded.

"I wasn't *spying*," Heather said. "I was actually just trying to be considerate."

"You want to be considerate? Leave!"

"Look, I know you hate me," Heather said, moving forward. "But you need to get over it."

"*You* get over it!" Marissa snapped, and immediately wished she hadn't because not only did it sound childish, it didn't make any sense.

Still. It *felt* right because Heather was so . . . Heather.

And her being there was so . . . *wrong*.

But Heather wasn't leaving. She was now standing on the opposite side of Sammy's bed, and had (to Marissa's horror) reached over the safety rail to hold Sammy's hand. "All that stuff you were talking about?" Heather said as she looked at Sammy. "We need to make a list."

Marissa was fixated on the hands. "A list of *what*?"

Heather turned to face her. "A list of people Sammy busted."

Marissa was dying to tell her it was a stupid idea. It was Heather's idea, after all, so it was, by definition, either stupid or evil.

Probably both.

Plus another knee-jerk retort was dying to shoot out of her mouth: Well, you'd take up the first ten slots, wouldn't you?!

But the words didn't come out because Marissa immediately knew that Heather's idea *wasn't* stupid.

It was a great idea.

One the police should have already thought of.

But before she could figure out how to agree with Heather without actually *agreeing* with Heather, Heather gasped.

"What?" Marissa asked, because the redhead's eyes were stretched wide.

"She . . . she . . ." Heather blinked across the bed at Marissa. "I think she just squeezed my hand!"

Marissa pounced forward to grab Sammy's other hand. "Sammy! Can you hear me?" She waited, and when there was no response, she shook her friend's shoulder. "Sammy!"

But again there was no response.

No squeeze.

Not even a twitch.

And after a few more attempts at getting a response—any kind of response—all that remained were dashed hopes and the awful suspicion that, once again, Heather was lying.

8—RANKLED

After the nursing staff had concluded that there was no evidence (other than Heather's word) that Sammy had actually moved, the teens gathered in the ICU waiting room, where Heather switched gears, announcing, "I'm going to go talk to the police about making a list."

Well, Marissa was not about to let Heather do that without her, so she immediately said, "I'm going, too."

"Are we tracking down the Borschman?" Casey asked.

Marissa nodded. "There are a lot of people Sammy helped put in jail. Maybe one of them did this to her."

Billy jumped up. "I'm in!"

"Us, too!" Holly and Dot said, and suddenly they were off, whooshing out of the waiting room and along the hallways in a gust of purpose, arriving at the steel elevator door just as it was whooshing open.

And this little dust devil of teenagers would have whooshed right into the elevator and down to the lobby, but they found themselves temporarily blocked by two people (and a large camera) intent on whooshing *out* of the elevator.

"That's Zelda Quinn!" Marissa gasped after the KSMY

reporter and her beleaguered cameraman had pushed through them and were hurrying down the corridor toward the ICU.

Holly shook her head. "Oh, this is bad."

"Very bad," Dot agreed.

And it certainly had that potential. With a dramatic streak of white hair traversing an otherwise jet-black coif, Zelda Quinn was a very recognizable presence in the community, ferreting out stories or, on slow news days, fanning smoky wisps of gossip into sizzling segments that she passed off as news.

And, having been temporarily forced out of the market by the smooth-talking (and conservatively coiffed) Grayson Mann, only to be reinstated after Mann's career meltdown and subsequent lockup, Zelda Quinn still harbored feelings of insecurity that (in a classic case of overcompensation) resulted in over-the-top reporting. Zelda Quinn wanted stories with flair! A sense of urgency and drama! And this story certainly had that. Plus the godsend of a celebrity connection!

Ratings would be through the roof!

Los Angeles markets might even see her!

And there was that elusive Emmy she'd always dreamed of accepting.

So Zelda Quinn had big plans to get to the bottom of what she had dubbed (without thought to alternate interpretations) the "Girl Hurled" story, and those plans included getting an interview with (or at least some really fine footage of) that hunka-hunka heartthrob Darren Cole.

Even if that meant camping out at the hospital.

Or breaking a few silly rules.

The public had a right to know!

So. Zelda whooshed down the hallway to pursue an Emmy, while Marissa and the others whooshed down the elevator to pursue Sergeant Borsch.

Which left Sammy in Room 411, all alone.

Down in the cafeteria, Rita was quickly approaching a breaking point. After Darren and Lana had joined her and Hudson, Lana had revved back into diva overdrive, complaining about everything from the coffee to the air-conditioning (which was, admittedly, on the chilly side), to the hospital's "complete and utter disregard for a parent's agony."

"Stop!" Rita finally begged her daughter. "This isn't helping anything!"

"She's just worried," Darren said as he texted a friend of a friend of a neurosurgeon at Stanford.

"And I'm not?" Rita snapped.

"Oh, forgive me for not wanting to chitchat about the weather!" Lana snapped back.

"I barely mentioned it!"

"And I barely mentioned the air-conditioning! Which anyone can tell is set to subzero!"

Rita turned to Hudson and said, "I need some fresh air."

Lana gave a little snort. "Isn't that typical?" She turned to Darren. "You wonder how I got so good at running away from my problems?" She pointed to Rita. "There's your answer!"

"That does it!" Rita said, standing up. "It's time you stopped blaming *me* for all your problems and took a good hard look in the mirror!"

"Me?" Lana squeaked. "How about *you*? You were *so* strict with me, but you let Samantha run wild!" She leaned in closer to her mother. "Why do you think we're in this predicament?"

Rita's jaw dropped.

Her cheeks flushed.

And finally alarms began clanging in both Darren's and Hudson's brains.

This was more than another mother-daughter spat.

This was serious!

"Fresh air sounds like a very good idea," Hudson said, moving his sputtering wife toward the exit.

"Lana's just exhausted and worried," Darren called apologetically.

"And I'm not?" Rita spat out. "But you don't hear me blaming *her* for this."

"Me?" Lana cried. "Me? How could you possibly blame me?"

And, incredulous right back, Rita took off the kid gloves and let the verbal knuckles fly. "Where have you been for the past *three years*? Seeing that your child was safe and secure and tucked in every night? No! You were too busy pampering your overblown ego!"

"My *what*?!"

Hudson cut in, calling, "We'll meet you upstairs in a while," as he swept Rita out the door.

"Can you believe her?" Rita cried when they were

outside. "After everything I've done to help her live her dream, this is the way she looks at things?"

"She feels guilty," Hudson said quietly, keeping his arm around his wife as they walked along.

"No, she doesn't! She's pointing the finger at *me*."

"You're her scapegoat, sweetheart," Hudson said. "She knows that she's done a lot wrong—it's just too painful to face."

"So she'd rather point the finger at me?"

"It's *easier* to point the finger at you." He gave his wife's shoulder a little squeeze. "You have every right to be mad. But I almost pity her, Rita. She missed so much."

They walked along, silent but for the *click-click-click* of Rita's heels on the sidewalk.

Which soon became the (somewhat duller-sounding) *click-click-click* of Rita's heels on asphalt.

"Where are we going?" Hudson asked, because his wife was now walking in that determined way that women do when they have something urgent to take care of.

"I need to change my clothes," Rita said, beelining toward Hudson's car.

"But . . . what's wrong with what you're wearing?"

Rita replied with the mantra of women everywhere: "My shoes are all wrong."

"Your shoes?"

"Yes," Rita cried (and she was now also crying), "my shoes!"

Hudson said, "Ah," then drove her home, where Rita switched into jeans as he located the red high-tops Sammy had given her the year before.

Rita wept the whole time she was changing, but as she snugged up her shoelaces, her eyes began to dry, and by the time the second shoe was pulled tight and the laces tucked away (as she'd seen Sammy do nearly every day of her teen life), she'd found another reserve of strength.

"To the Highrise," she said with her chin pushed resolutely forward.

And although Hudson really wanted to ask, "Uh . . . why?" he again simply drove her where she wanted to go.

"Park here," Rita instructed, a full block from the building, then led her husband on a long walk around the Highrise to the fire escape.

"I'm surprised the area isn't cordoned off as a crime scene," Hudson said. And as his wife started up the fire-escape stairs, he couldn't help but ask, "Are you sure you want to do this?"

"Positive," Rita replied.

When they reached the third-floor landing, the pair looked over the edge. And when Rita began visibly shivering, Hudson wrapped her in his arms and said, "Why are we here?"

But Rita simply shook her head and dug down for strength. Then she checked the third-floor door (which was locked and latched) and went up to the fourth floor. "This is the spot where she scared that man to death," she said, referring to a night Sammy had surprised a man with a weak heart and a guilty conscience as he'd tried to slip out of the building unnoticed. "That was quite a night."

"You do this like a pro," Hudson said as they continued up to the fifth floor.

"I've been up and down a few times," she replied, then looked over her shoulder at him. "Mostly the time Lana let Samantha's cat escape."

At the fifth-floor landing, Hudson looked back down the way they'd come. "The reality of this is much different from the theory," he remarked. And after a moment of visualizing Sammy using the fire escape, day and night, to school and back, to the market and back, to the mall and back, to his house and back, for *years,* he asked, "How did she do this in the rain?"

Rita stood beside him and looked over the railing— a terrifying view. "She never complained," she said, moving away from the edge. "She just did it."

"And the door?" Hudson asked, turning around to face it. "How'd it stay unlocked?"

"Bubblegum," Rita said, pulling it open and showing him the large, pale pink wad in the jamb. "The door looks and feels locked, but it's not latched."

Hudson studied it a moment. "Shouldn't we remove the bubblegum, now that you no longer live here?"

But there was something about the secret back entry that Rita wasn't ready to let go of. Something about knowing she could come and go as she pleased, without notice or questioning. It was more than a matter of holding on to the past.

It was the sheer sleuthiness of it.

Although what, exactly, she was sleuthing, she didn't know. Clearly, there was nothing to be seen regarding what had happened to Samantha. And why else would she want to be there?

Still, removing her granddaughter's bubblegum was like voluntarily closing up a secret passageway. A passageway that suddenly reminded her of things she'd read about in books as a youth. Like a revolving bookcase that led to a labyrinth of secret hallways and spying portals. Or the hidden door behind a heavy velvet curtain! Or the floor panel under the old rug that exposed a staircase going down, down, down . . . !

Granted, this was just a steel door into a decrepit building full of old people, but it was as close to a secret passageway as she'd ever come.

So Rita simply said, "Not yet," in response to Hudson's question and led him down the hallway to where her old apartment awaited its new resident. "This is very strange," she whispered, hesitating at the apartment door.

They stood there for a full minute, and when he just couldn't stand it anymore, Hudson asked, "Is there a reason we're here?"

Now, not knowing that Sergeant Borsch had done almost the exact same tour hours before, Rita determined that the best course of action was to knock on neighbors' doors and ask a few questions.

So that's what she did. But unlike the encounter Gil Borsch had had with twitching noses and squeaking voices, Rita was assaulted with full views of her former neighbors and a flurry of accusations and cutting remarks.

"What are *you* doing back here?"

"Oh, look. It's the bride."

"Get a load of those shoes. She must think she's a hipster or something."

"You never once knocked on my door before, and now you expect me to give you information?"

"Just ask the police, why don't you?"

"Yeah. That pork belly was here earlier."

"Or watch the news. It's all over the news."

And then the conversation switched. Instead of the neighbors directing what they said at Rita, they started talking to each other as if Rita and Hudson weren't even there.

"Who was that girl, anyway?"

"They didn't say."

"But her father's someone famous."

"He is? Who?"

"They didn't come out and say, but that Zelda Quinn's hyperventilating about it. And apparently the mother was on a soap."

"Do you think it might have been *Lords*?"

"Could be."

"Why in the world did they end that show, anyway?"

"Who knows? You see what's on TV now. Ridiculous smut."

"But . . . who was she on the show?"

"I already told you. They didn't say. It was a teaser. The full story comes on tonight."

"On KSMY?"

"Yes."

"I had no idea there were any celebrities in Santa Martina!"

"Not unless you count Mayor Hibbs."

"Oh, he *thinks* he's a celebrity."

"He has such a paunch these days, have you noticed?"

"Our tax dollars, hard at work."

"Forget about the mayor! If there are real celebrities in town, I have to tune in!"

"Me, too!"

"Say, I have some vin rosé left in my box—I could bring it over later."

"I have a can of olives!"

"I can bring crackers!"

"Let's do it! My place! Five o'clock!" Then this hostess with the mostest turned a harsh eye on Rita and said, "Residents only," and closed her door.

Suddenly alone in a quiet hallway, Rita took a deep breath and said, "Why do I feel like I'm back in school?"

Hudson chuckled. "Clearly, they have yet to graduate." He kissed her temple, then said, "Shall we go?"

Rita nodded, but rather than go out the way they'd come in, she said, "Let's take a shortcut."

Hudson laughed again. "Sounds appropriate."

So they went down the hallway to the elevator, and down the elevator to the basement, where Rita was planning to lead Hudson down a corridor to a side exit. If her former neighbors hadn't conveyed that a policeman had already been there, she would have braved the booming voice and good-intentioned questioning of Mr. Garnucci, but she saw no reason to do so now.

And had Rita been alone, she would likely not have gone down to the basement exit. Once past the laundry facility, the corridor was dim, and the exit itself was in a somewhat remote location. Rita had only ventured out of it once before, when she'd run out of fabric softener while doing her laundry.

But she had Hudson with her now, and the route made sense because the basement exit would let them out near the place Hudson had parked the car. And everything would have been fine and straightforward had Rita not peered through the laundry-room doorway and noticed the furtive movements of someone digging through an open dryer.

In the instant it takes to put two and two together, Rita grabbed Hudson's arm and pulled him out of sight, then inched forward to peer around the doorway.

"What is it?" Hudson whispered.

"Shh," Rita replied, not quite believing what she was seeing. But after another few seconds of observation, she went from shock to certainty. "Quick," she whispered to Hudson. "We need to call Sergeant Borsch!"

9—ODD DUCKS

While Rita and Hudson were sidetracked by their shocking discovery in the Highrise basement and the six-pack of teens were across town attempting to track down Sergeant Borsch, Lana's stress level was being pushed to an all-time high.

"*Marko's* here?" she asked Darren in a way that was both accusatory and derogatory.

To Darren's surprise, the drummer for the Troublemakers had, indeed, just entered the cafeteria. With his shaved head and the piratey look of a rock star, there was no mistaking him, and with him came (for Darren) a sense of enormous relief.

Now, this was not the complete relief Darren would have felt had he just learned that Sammy was going to be okay. Rather, this was the shoulder-lifting, burden-sharing sort of relief that comes with friendship.

A friendship forged by childhood adventures (and misadventures) and decades of being (both metaphorically and musically) Troublemakers.

"Dude!" Marko cried when he spotted his best friend. And after dropping the bag he was carrying so he could wrap Darren in a long (somewhat crushing) man hug, he pulled back and asked, "She hasn't come to?"

Darren shook his head.

Marko studied his best friend a moment and recognized that Darren was dancing on the edge of despair. So he got to work shoring him up. "But it hasn't even been twenty-four hours, right? And she's a pint-sized prizefighter, right? So she's going to pull out of it." He clasped Darren by the shoulders. "Dude, she is going to pull out of it!"

The thing about a best friend is that they manage to carry authority without knowledge. You believe them, even if they have no idea what they're talking about. Largely, this is because you *want* to believe them, and partly it's because they've spoken authoritatively about things in the past that they've also had no actual knowledge of, and they've turned out to be right.

In friendship (especially those of the male variety), a few tallies in the Right column easily overpower a plethora of points in the Wrong column.

That's just how it is.

The upshot of this being that Darren immediately felt better.

Lana, not so much.

The sad fact was, Lana had no friend like Marko. No sister *or* sis-ta. Any overtures of friendship from other young mothers had been met with a detached coolness.

Lana'd had plans beyond the jungle gym.

She'd needed to focus on her goals.

And once she'd returned to Hollywood, she'd found

she needed to focus even harder. It was impossible to trust competing actors, and every role seemed to become a ruthless competition.

It was also hard to make friends when you were hiding your real age, your embarrassing past, and the fact that you had a teenage daughter.

So Marko's sudden appearance at the hospital was, for Lana, a reminder of what she'd sacrificed.

Plus, Marko was . . . childish.

And always tapping on things.

And how many times could a grown man say "Dude!" anyway?

Lana knew better than to express her disapproval at the Troublemaking intrusion . . . but then came the shoes.

"Dude, you're gonna want to have these on when she wakes up," Marko said, handing over the bag he'd brought. And when Darren saw that the bag contained the high-tops Sammy had given him, he immediately sat down, wrestled out of his boots, and laced on the shoes.

Lana knew that these shoes had been customized by Sammy—"scribbled on" by her with little sayings and inside jokes. They were very similar to the shoes Casey had given Sammy for her fourteenth birthday, and they were, in a word, ugly.

(And in another word, childish.)

(And in a third, ridiculous.)

(And in a . . . Well, it was best not to get her started.)

The bottom line was that Lana just didn't get it. Not about high-tops (which seemed flat, ill-fitting, and with their clownlike extension in the toe, not at all flattering), or the need to deface with Sharpies something that was ugly to begin with.

So with the shoes out of the bag, the disapproving vibe coming off of Lana was now palpable.

But Darren (being both male and in the presence of his best bro) was oblivious. "So glad you're here, man," he said as he grasped Marko in another quick hug.

"Can I see her?" Marko asked quietly. "I'd really like to see her."

"Yeah, let's go," Darren said, then held Lana's hand as the threesome made their way back to the ICU.

Across town, a flamboyant resident at the Heavenly Hotel had seen the KSMY teaser regarding a girl hurled from the third-floor fire escape of the Senior Highrise. A fortune-teller by trade, Madame (Gina) Nashira had felt a distinct chill pass through her during the short segment, not simply because of the horrific act, but because she immediately had a suspicion as to who the girl might be.

So after frantically consulting the previous day's horoscope for Aries, she snatched up her purse (and a pack of cigarettes) and, not wanting to waste time on the hotel's dilapidated elevator, jangled down four mind-bending mirror-flanked flights of stairs to the Heavenly Hotel lobby.

"André!" she cried at the manager, who was behind the counter, an unlit cigar stub clamped between his teeth as he concentrated on punching numbers into a calculator.

"We on fire?" the manager growled without looking up.

"When's the last time you've seen Sammy?"

Now André looked up. And to his surprise, he found he was dealing with one of his more sane (and financially responsible) residents.

Ordinarily, Madame Nashira was a cool character. Draped in scarves and jingling with jewelry, she spoke of astral planes and cosmic coordinates, and there was nothing like her mysterious coo to make a man part with a few bucks for a palm reading.

But at the moment the coo was gone, and there was more than simple panic in her eyes.

There was full-blown fear.

"It's been a couple of days," André replied carefully. "Why?"

So Gina blurted out what she'd seen on the news, then cried, "Yesterday's horoscope for Aries was 'Avoid heights and stay close to home. Danger lurks in the shadows.'" Her eyes widened even farther. "Sammy's an Aries!"

André was (to put it mildly) a skeptic when it came to Gina's astral forecasts and fortune-telling. He considered it mumbo-jumbo. Bogus. A fool's folly.

The word *stupid* also came to mind.

After all, Gina had once assured him that a woman was about to enter his life. She'd had a vision. One that included him and a woman who embodied "true heart and humor."

And homemade lasagna.

"I could almost smell it," she'd cooed. "The garlic? The oregano? My mouth was waterin'!"

Gina hadn't charged him for relaying the vision, and it

81

was a good thing, too, because it had been six months and no woman of true heart *or* humor had entered his life. Nor had there been any signs of homemade lasagna—which was the part of Gina's vision that had intrigued André the most.

So the horoscope would ordinarily not have rung any alarms in André's mind, but the combination of the news, the horoscope, and the uncharacteristic concern in both Gina's voice and her streetwise eyes caused the hotel manager to do more than just roll his cigar stub to one side of his mouth to facilitate better communication.

He actually removed it.

"What are you sayin'?" he asked the fortune-teller.

So Gina repeated everything she'd already said.

The upside to managing a run-down hotel is that you become familiar with local law enforcement. They're in a lot. They get to know you. They learn not to blame you for your clientele, and begin to empathize with your plight.

After all, you don't *own* the place. You just work there. And who would want to spend their days (and nights) in a place that smelled like rotten potatoes, squeezing rent out of derelicts and drunks?

So André was on a first-name basis with a number of people at the police station, and he managed (after several phone transfers) to confirm that the girl who'd been hurled from the fire escape of the Senior Highrise was, indeed, Samantha Keyes.

"It's her," he told Gina once he hung up. And while the fortune-teller whimpered and paced and cursed on one side of the counter, André turned back to the phone and called Community Hospital from the other side.

Unfortunately, he knew no one at the hospital. ODs and stabbings funneled from the Heavenly had done nothing to build a rapport between the hotel manager and hospital personnel. If anything, the opposite was true.

So extracting information about Sammy's condition was impossible.

There were rules.

And André wasn't "family."

"You don't understand," he tried to explain, because what was family, anyway?

A diva mom who was never there?

Or the people who loved the kid and all the trouble that came along with her?

Roadblocked, André finally slammed down the phone. And having no viable option, he did something that Gina, in all her years at the Heavenly, had never witnessed.

He locked up anything valuable (or remotely pawnable), grabbed his keys, and growled, "Let's go."

Once outside the hotel, they were stopped in their tracks by a muscle-bound man wearing tight black shorts, a yellow racerback tank, and bright blue wrestling boots. "Hey . . . !" the man called as he locked the door to Slammin' Dave's Pro Wrestling School. And that's where the greeting stalled because, despite their having been neighbors for over a year, the school's owner did not know the hotel manager's name. What he *did* know was that his young friend Sammy hung out at the Heavenly (although why, he'd never really understood), and that a rumor had flown through the wrestling school that she'd taken a bump that even a world-class wrestler would have trouble surviving. "Is it true?"

André had heard tales from Sammy about Slammin' Dave and his pro wrestling school, so although the two men had never spoken, André understood exactly what the wrestler was asking. "Looks like," he said through his cigar stub. "We're headin' over to the hospital now." And then, in a flash of camaraderie that only shared despair can produce, he asked, "Want a ride?"

Slammin' Dave nodded. "Thanks, man."

Then off they went.

Pedal to the metal.

Three odd and weathered ducks, praying for a way to rescue their town's bravest (and dearest) duckling.

10—A MENAGERIE

Like the blind calling out to the deaf for help, the six-pack of teens was getting nowhere fast. At the police station they were told that Sergeant Borsch had gone to the Highrise. At the Highrise they checked both the crime scene and the lobby and found no sign of him, or the manager.

"That's weird," Casey said. "I thought that Garnucci guy was always here."

They stood around the quiet lobby for a minute, and finally Holly asked, "Well, where to now?"

Marissa shrugged. "Back to the police station?"

"Why don't we just call?" Heather snapped, but since it was Heather asking and she was being bossy, Marissa, Holly, and Dot simply began walking toward the police station.

So Billy told Heather, "Come on, let's just go," and Casey added, "It's on the way back to the hospital."

But at the police station they were informed that, although Sergeant Borsch *had* been there a little while ago, he was gone again now.

"See?" Heather said as they left the station. "We should have called."

The other girls couldn't ignore the fact that she was right, but they did their best to do so anyway. "He's probably at the hospital," Holly said. "I'm heading back there."

"Me, too," Marissa said.

Heather, however, was getting fed up with the senselessness of the trek. "What are we *doing*? We should have just stayed at the hospital if this is all we're doing!"

And although to Dot it *was* reminiscent of Pooh Bear and friends aimlessly circling the Hundred Acre Wood, she didn't voice that comparison. Instead, she diplomatically suggested, "We didn't know when we set out that we'd wind up back at the start. Sometimes you have to go nowhere to get somewhere."

The others mentally scratched their heads at that comment, but Heather just came out and said, *"What?"*

"You know what I mean," Dot said, which elicited from Marissa and Holly a decisive "Of course we do!" and made Casey murmur to his sister, "Just walk."

"But—"

"Just walk."

So walk they did.

Until they entered the hospital's front parking lot, where they all stopped dead in their tracks.

"Is that . . . ?" Marissa said, pointing to a battered dirt bike with a sidecar. But with the red pennant flag sporting a big gold *J*, there was really no mistaking the vehicle.

"Justice Jack is *back*," Billy squealed, and took off running toward the hospital.

"Oh, Officer Borsch is going to love this," Marissa grumbled as they all hurried after Billy.

Marissa's sarcasm wasn't without cause. From his Golden Gloves of Justice to his Pellets of Pain . . . *t,* Jack Wesley—known to his regional fans as the red-and-gold-spandex-clad Justice Jack—was one do-gooder that Sergeant Borsch had been happy to see relocate to a town far, far away.

Billy, on the other hand, had missed him. Having done a stint as the Deuce alongside the wannabe superhero, Billy had found an escape from the darker aspects of his life. Justice Jack had served as a mentor. Someone who held high ideals, expressed a courageous optimism, and could uncover a silver lining in even the most thunderous clouds.

Someone Billy embraced for being very much *not* like his father.

"Jack!" Billy cried as he charged into the ICU waiting room and spotted Jack Wesley in full regalia. "I thought you'd hung up the mask for good!"

"Some things in life are worth a reboot," Jack boomed, stomping one of his thickly leathered (and heavily buckled) feet. "And capturing the culprit who did this despicable deed is just such a thing!"

"But . . . how'd you hear? I thought you'd moved to Reno!"

Jack didn't want to let on that, although his training at the police academy in Reno was going fairly well, he still monitored law enforcement activities in Santa Martina because, let's face it, change is hard, and hanging up the Golden Gloves of Justice and the red-and-gold bodysuit for a conservative blue uniform with a few staid patches was even harder. (And don't even bring up how he'd had to cut off his long hair.)

So he simply boomed, "It was a long trip, little shaver, but worth every mile!" as he punched his fists against the sides of his superhero-inspired utility belt.

It was at this point that Billy noticed the hair. On a regular long-haired Joe, it would have been the first thing anyone would notice, but with Jack it took a few minutes to process past the black mask and Roman centurion helmet. And Billy was about to exclaim, "Dude, you cut your hair!" only in that brief period of processing it also occurred to him that they were on camera. Although set up in a side room, a large news camera was pointed directly at them, and the red light was definitely on.

"Cut!" Zelda Quinn instructed her cameraman because Billy was now glowering in her direction. And then three other individuals charged into the waiting room, completely pulling the reporter's focus away from Justice Jack and the glowering teen.

First there was a woman whose hair was ratted and shellacked to unbelievable heights. She was flowing with silk (and synthetic) scarves and wearing lots of dangling, jangling jewelry (all costume, save one silver-plated watch).

Right behind her was a man wearing ridiculously tight shorts, sky-blue wrestling boots, and a tank top that barely covered his bulging chest. And following *him* was a stout man with greased-back hair and a cigar stub clamped between his teeth, looking for all the world like he'd just stepped off the set of a 1930s gangster movie.

And when the trio all skidded to a halt and gasped,

"What's the news on Sammy?" Zelda Quinn knew beyond a shadow of a doubt that she had hit the mother lode. Whoever this girl was (besides the daughter of a legendary rock star, of course) and whatever she'd been doing on the fire escape of the Senior Highrise, there was a story here.

A big, big story.

Full of weird, weird people.

It was a reporter's dream!

But she had to be careful. Unobtrusive. To get permission to be there at all, she'd had to plead her case to a hospital administrator, citing a desire to rally the community and capture a (maybe) kid killer. Still, it was only after making a host of confining promises (which included stringent stipulations involving patients' privacy and not disturbing other people in the waiting room) that she'd been allowed to stay.

So Zelda Quinn was surrounded by lines that could not be crossed, but she was not one to be contained by lines. She'd learned long ago that subject footage coupled with her own voice-overs made for a more efficient use of airtime anyway. She could get to the point succinctly, without the notorious time-chewing *um*'s or *you know*'s typical of interviewees.

Yes, she knew how to work around the constraints imposed by the hospital, and from the way the oddball adults were now in animated conversation with what were clearly the Hurled Girl's friends, Zelda Quinn gathered her resolve.

It was time to mingle!

"Rolling?" she asked her cameraman under her breath.

"You said cut," he said back.

"Well, roll!" she said through her teeth. "And keep on rolling!" Then she stepped over the line (invisible though it was) and entered the fray. "Excuse me," she said, and when the oddball adults and six-pack of teens fell silent, she told them, "I want to help."

Good newscasters convince you they care. With attentive head bobbing and sympathetic eye contact, they pull a story along, ostensibly siding with their subject until a certain comfort level is reached and they are able to skillfully extract disquieting nuggets of emotion or controversial statements. Ideally, both.

Novice subjects allow this to happen. (In other words, they get worked.) An experienced subject, on the other hand (like, say, a politician), is always on point, rarely derailed, and gives (in the eyes of journalists and viewers alike) miserable interviews.

Of all the people in the conglomeration of oddball adults and teens, the only one not at least somewhat mesmerized by Zelda Quinn and her conjured sincerity was Holly. And after a minute or so of feigned tolerance, she slipped away, unnoticed, and made her way to Room 411.

Holly was relieved to get to Sammy's room undeterred, but as she went inside, she was practically knocked over by an orderly on his way out.

"Oh, excuse me!" Holly gasped.

"That's okay!" the orderly said as he maneuvered around her.

"How is she?" Holly called after him, but he was already gone.

And then she saw Sammy's bed and panic engulfed her.

Two nuns and a priest were standing over the bed, praying.

"No!" Holly cried, sure that they were giving last rites.

"Don't be alarmed," one of the nuns said. And that's when Holly noticed that the other nun had a big black cane and that this threesome was none other than Sisters Mary Margaret and Josephine and the bumbling Brother Phil. She hadn't seen them in over a year, but they'd served her many times at the soup kitchen. Back when she'd been living on the streets.

"Come, child," Sister Mary Margaret said (addressing her in the way nuns do when they don't recall a person's name). "Father Mayhew told us about Samantha. We thought prayer was in order."

"Oh," Holly said, greatly relieved.

"We've also been reminiscing with Samantha," Sister Josephine added, and now Holly noticed that each sister was holding one of Sammy's hands.

"About the Sisters of Mercy," Brother Phil said from the foot of the bed. "We were just getting to the part where Sammy crashed their motor home."

"Into a police car!" Mary Margaret exclaimed.

The cluster of clergy laughed at this memory. Not in a dignified manner, as you might expect from people of the cloth, but in a chortling, sniggering, tittering way.

Sister Mary Margaret, especially, seemed to relish the memory. "You did good, sweetheart," she said to Sammy, then kissed her on the forehead.

"God has a plan for you, Samantha," Sister Josephine said, and she, too, kissed her on the forehead.

"Let's hope that plan includes her wakin' up," Brother Phil said, and although he said it under his breath, the nuns heard him.

"When are you going to learn to give things over to God?" Sister Mary Margaret chided him.

"When she wakes up," Brother Phil muttered.

"Better get to your prayers, then," Sister Josephine said with a frown.

"Well," Sister Mary Margaret said to the others, "we've had more than our fair share of time with Samantha. Shall we?" Then the three of them bid Holly farewell and left the room.

"Wow," Holly said aloud as she took the seat next to Sammy's bed, "they haven't changed a bit, huh?" And although she was trying to sound upbeat, seeing the two sisters and Brother Phil reminded her of a past that wasn't at all cheery. A past when she had been hungry and alone, stealing to survive, and living in a cardboard box down by the riverbed.

And, flashing back to that time, Holly suddenly broke down and sobbed, "I don't know where I'd be if you hadn't dragged me over to Meg and Vera's. My whole life has changed because of you. If you hadn't followed me home from the soup kitchen, if you hadn't stopped that guy from . . . from probably *killing* me . . . if you hadn't helped me fit in at school . . . if you hadn't . . . Sammy, *please*. You've got to wake up!"

But Sammy just lay there.

Which made Holly cry even harder.

And the harder Holly cried, the worse she felt. She was back to being helpless and hopeless and fearful and vulnerable—all things she'd rallied so hard against.

And then a hand stroked her back and a soothing voice said, "Hey . . . hey . . ." When she turned around, she found herself face to face with Sarah Rothhammer, the school's sometimes fierce (but always fair) science teacher.

Holly's immediate reaction was that she was in trouble.

She had, after all, ditched school.

"What time is it?" she asked, wondering if school had already let out.

"Almost one o'clock. And don't worry," Ms. Rothhammer said (clearly reading her mind). "I found people to cover my last two classes, but if you ask me, school should have just been canceled today." Then she studied Sammy a minute and addressed her directly. "No homework tonight, Sammy. I gave everyone the night off in your honor. But tomorrow? Tomorrow you need to be back with us, okay? I can't have you falling behind after all the progress you've made catching up." And then dropping her voice to speak to Holly again, she asked, "Have they given any indication when she might wake up?"

Holly shook her head. "It's all wait-and-see. But I know the longer this goes on, the worse it is."

Sarah Rothhammer gave a knowing nod. She didn't mean to, but scientific sensibilities controlled her head, and her head was closer to her neck than it was to her heart. So the nod confirmed Holly's statement before she could consider its emotional impact. But then, seeing her normally

93

stoic student's new wave of tears, she quickly added, "But it's early still—give her a chance." And then, in an effort to turn the mood around, she addressed Sammy again with "You wouldn't believe what a commotion you've caused. The waiting room's a zoo! I've never seen anything like it!"

"Yeah," Holly said, catching on. "Madame Nashira's out there. And so is Slammin' Dave. And André. And Justice Jack! Jack says he's ready to give whoever did this to you a tour of Stomp City!"

"And all your friends are out there, too," Sarah added. "Including the miraculously converted Heather Acosta." She shook her head. "You have to tell me what you did to that girl. I thought she was a goner, but what a turnaround." Then she eyed Holly and said, "I hope."

"Yeah," Holly said with a frown. "I'm not a true believer yet."

The science teacher laughed. "It'll take all of us a while, I think." Then she shifted gears, saying, "I was surprised I could even get up here to the room, but nobody stopped me, or even questioned me. Maybe because of all the commotion?"

But security concerns were immediately forgotten as a primordial squeal emanated from a nurse mid-hallway.

Fortunately, it was not a squeal of pain or danger.

It was a squeal of sheer delight.

Darren Cole had entered the ICU.

11—TEDDY BEARS

The delay in Darren getting from the cafeteria to the ICU was not Lana's doing.

It was Marko's.

"Dude!" he'd suddenly said as they were waiting for the elevator. "I need to bring Sammy something."

"She's unconscious," Darren reminded him.

"But she's gonna wake up! And when she does, there needs to be something from her uncle Marko! Right there! Center front!"

"Her uncle Marko?" Lana choked out, and the already present knot in her stomach tightened.

There was, in fact, no biological relationship between Sammy and the drummer, but Lana's reaction stemmed from the clear (and painful) truth:

Sammy liked Marko.

Really-really liked him.

And it was clear (and also painful) to Lana that Sammy *didn't* like her.

Really-really *didn't* like her.

So as Lana and Darren followed Marko to the gift shop, Lana's eyes filled with tears, which Darren noticed.

"She's going to be all right," the rocker said, wrapping an arm around her. "We have to believe she's going to be all right."

Lana just shook her head, and Darren (to his credit) could see that there was something more on her mind. He stopped, letting Marko go into the gift shop alone. "What is it?" he asked softly.

So with the swipe of a spilled tear and a little cringe, Lana confessed, "I feel so left out."

"Left out?"

"She's only known you and Marko a few months, and it's like she's known you her whole life. Me she's known her whole life, but we're practically strangers. She doesn't want to do anything with me, she'll barely text me back, and she never returns my calls. But you? You're like her best friend!"

Darren looked away and tried not to acknowledge the truth in Lana's words. "Well, we took that cruise together and—"

"That's not it. You two just *clicked*. You laugh and joke and talk for hours. Do you realize how long you're on the phone with her? And Marko's got that same ease with her. But me? I feel like I'm in the way. I'm uptight and no fun and too worried about every little thing." She gave him a pleading look. "I know Marko hates that I'm back in your life."

"He does not."

"Oh, Darren . . ."

Darren studied her a moment, then gathered some resolve. "Look, he knows you make *me* happy." He dropped his voice even further. "But it would help if you could relax a little around him. . . . Maybe try not to be so disapproving of his, you know . . . youthful qualities?"

Lana cringed. "It's that obvious?"

Darren laughed. "Yes, my love."

She cringed harder. "With Samantha, too?"

Now, a weak (or cowardly) man would have lied. Or given a diplomatic (or spineless) response. But Darren Cole was not fainthearted, so out came the simple truth. "Yes."

Rather than be defensive (which would have been a very natural reaction and almost *required* of a more seasoned diva), Lana instead broke down. "Why am I like that? I don't *want* to be judgmental. I don't *want* to be uptight. It just . . . it just happens!"

Darren gave her a scrutinizing look. "Are we really discussing this right now?"

"Yes!"

"Okay, then." He thought for a few seconds, then just came out with it. "Marko thinks it's because you're insecure."

"*Marko* does?" Lana asked, arching an eyebrow.

The archy eyebrow (although a small gesture) elicited a big reaction from Darren. "That right there?" he said (pointing to the archy eyebrow). "That's condescending. Marko is a smart guy. He may be a child at heart, but that's part of his intelligence. He knows how to connect with the truth." He calmed himself with a deep breath, then continued. "You need people around you who keep you anchored to the truth, Lana."

"But . . . how can he think I'm a diva—which I know he does—and say I'm insecure?"

Darren gave her a wry smile. "In our experience they usually go together."

"What?"

"It's true! It's an overcompensation thing." But since Lana was obviously not buying what he was saying, he sighed and explained, "Look, you were basically a kid when you had Sammy. And I was off being an oblivious rock star, which I'm sure made you feel abandoned and betrayed and all of that. Then your dad bailed on your mom for some biker chick because he couldn't take the idea of being a grandpa, and he crashed his Harley and died. So you felt abandoned and betrayed and *guilty,* and you've spent all the years since then trying to be perfect to prove you could rise above the . . . mess." He looked at her directly. "But real life *is* messy. Being perfect *won't* change the past. And it won't get you anywhere real."

Lana looked down, quiet. And after a long minute had gone by, she said, "All that from Marko?"

Darren hesitated. "Let's just say he set the rhythm and I put in the notes." Then he tipped up Lana's chin and said, "Those of us out front shouldn't undervalue the rock-solid people behind us." He looked into the gift shop. "Even if mine just bought seventeen stuffed bears."

"Dude!" Marko cried as he waddled out of the gift shop. And although it seemed impossible that he could see where he was going through all the synthetic fur he was hugging, he made a beeline for Darren and dumped his load of bears (along with a stowaway unicorn) at Darren's feet, then dashed back to the gift shop, where he retrieved a dozen helium balloons and a gift-shop bag containing Sharpie markers and rolls of extra-wide ribbon. "Flowers are not allowed in the ICU," he announced, then started picking up bears and shoving them at Darren. "Help me out, man!"

Lana wanted to tell the drummer that there was no room for seventeen stuffed bears (and a stowaway unicorn) in her daughter's room, but she bit her tongue. And while she was biting her tongue (and Darren was picking up bears), a bubble of regret percolated through her.

Did she really have to be uptight about teddy bears?

"Here, I'll carry some," she volunteered.

Now, the simple truth was, Lana had never been mistaken for a roadie. Or even a distant friend of a roadie. It was fully understood that Lana Keyes didn't carry stuff.

Well, her purse.

And boutique bags.

But guitars or amps or drums or even cables?

Her fingerprints on those were nowhere to be found.

And although teddy bears were certainly not guitars or amps or drums (or even cables), it was the simple act of volunteering to carry *anything* that stunned Marko. His arms froze. His eyes bugged. His jaw dropped.

And then, when Lana actually stooped down to pick up bears and said, "This is very sweet of you, Marko," it seemed that the rim-shot-slammin' drummer might just fall over.

Fortunately, he had a dozen helium balloons helping to keep him upright. "I'm thinkin' everyone can write a message," he explained (once his jaw was back in socket). "Her friends, her grandparents, us . . . maybe a teacher or two."

"Write a message?" Lana asked.

So Marko showed her the ribbons and the packs of Sharpie markers. "I'm thinkin' the bears could use some message bows, you know?"

Lana's eyes were suddenly stinging with tears. "Like the shoes," she choked out.

"Aw, Lana," Marko said, and he would have dropped everything to hug her, only he'd learned a long time ago that Lana Keyes was not the hugging type. So instead he simply said, "She's going to be okay, okay?"

"Please tell me that again," she said with a quivery smile.

"She's going to be okay, okay?"

Lana made a noise somewhere between a sniff and a laugh, then picked up the unicorn and said, "She is going to hate this one."

Marko gave Darren a quick look that clearly conveyed Uh-oh, because he'd picked out the unicorn specifically for Lana.

Something Lana had already figured out.

"I don't want to be a unicorn in a forest of bears," she said quietly.

"But a unicorn is a beautiful, magical creature," Marko said. Then he quickly added, "Besides, the surface on that is going to be awesome to write on. Check it out. See how smooth it is?"

Lana found herself laughing (in the best of ways) at

Marko's exuberance. And being considered beautiful and magical was not a *bad* thing.

Still. Beauty and magic didn't matter now unless she had some magic that would bring Sammy back.

Which she didn't.

And really, at this point, no other kind of magic mattered. She just wanted Sammy to wake up.

She wanted the chance to start over with her.

To relax and accept and . . . and appreciate.

So she took a deep breath and told Marko, "Maybe we'll get some of her friends to write on this one. I think I'd rather have a bear."

"All righty, then!" Marko said, giving Darren a very pleased bro-grin. "Let's get these woodland creatures up to Sammy!"

So off they went with their balloons and bears (and a stowaway unicorn) to the elevator and up to the ICU.

Which (with one skunk reporter, four odd ducks, and six testy teens) was (as Sarah Rothhammer was just sharing) already quite a zoo.

12—DIRTY LAUNDRY

Hudson and Rita weren't part of the waiting-room hub-bub, being instead sidetracked by the suspicious activities taking place inside the Highrise laundry room.

"Why in the world would we call Gil Borsch?" Hudson whispered after Rita suggested it.

"Because *that*," Rita said, "is the Nightie-Napper."

"Vince Garnucci is the Nightie-Napper?"

Now, ordinarily a man with a . . . let's just call it an *affinity* for old-ladies' nightgowns (or muumuus, or bed-sheets of floral design) would not seem like a threatening figure.

It was clear from his quick, furtive actions as he rummaged through the dryer and held up articles of clothing before tossing them back in that the Highrise manager was doing more than checking the moisture content of processed laundry. Still, to Hudson, a call to a psychiatrist seemed more appropriate than a call to the police.

But there *was* the unsettling issue of Holly's mention of Sammy's mention of the Nightie-Napper shortly before the attack.

And, slight as the man rummaging through the dryer was, maybe secrets of this sort brought out the beast inside.

Maybe there *was* danger in confronting him.

Especially since Rita no longer lived in the building and nobody knew they were there.

Now, please don't jump to the conclusion that Hudson Graham was wimping out.

He most certainly was not.

But Hudson Graham, being an intelligent man, was considering the options before springing into action. It was not in his DNA (or his CIA training) to call the police (or, for that matter, ask for help). It *was* in his nature (as well as his training) to handle things himself.

But he had just decided that a call to Sergeant Borsch would be wise when Rita suddenly stepped out from behind cover and into the laundry room.

"Vince!" Rita snapped as she moved quickly across the room. "All this time it's been *you*."

The dryers in the basement of the Senior Highrise are (like everything else in the building) old. They are giant tumblers with large, porthole-style doors that swing open for easy access (and are still only fifty cents for forty minutes).

"Rita!" Vince Garnucci gasped as he ditched a short-sleeved, 100 percent cotton, primrose-patterned nightgown into the dryer. "What brings you back to the Highrise?"

But Rita cut straight to the point. "All this time we residents suspected each other—but it was *you*."

"Me?" Vince Garnucci let out a forced laugh. "Rita, what are you talking about?"

"You know darned well what I'm talking about! You're the Nightie-Napper!"

"Me?" The manager produced another laugh. "I was just trying to figure out whose clothes these were so I could call and say they're done so the Nightie-Napper *won't* get them!"

It was true that some residents had taken to marking their names inside their garments to discourage their disappearance (which is never a bad practice in institutions where memories are slipping anyway), but Rita wasn't buying. "Nice try, Vince."

Rita had always been a lady around the building manager. A (comparatively) calm, level-headed lady. But she had a look in her eye now. A serious, you-are-*mine* look in her eye. And instead of ladylike shoes, she was wearing red, kick-tush shoes, and the combination was clearly throwing Vince Garnucci for a loop.

"Now, Rita," he said, backing away from her as she approached.

"Don't you now-Rita me! I know what I saw!"

"Why would I steal nightgowns?" the manager choked out, backpedaling as Rita chased him.

"For your grandmother!" Rita cried (because two plus two was definitely equaling four).

"Hudson!" the manager cried. "Stop her! This is all a misunderstanding!"

But Hudson knew a guilty man when he saw one and instead said, "Give it up, m'man."

Panic flashed across Vince Garnucci's face. But rather

than just give it up (as well he should have), he continued moving backward, praying for a way out.

Instead, he found a way *in*.

Into an open dryer, that is.

The minute he crashed into it and stumbled backward, Rita pounced forward, shoved him in the rest of the way (swinging his legs around with a mighty heave-ho), and closed the door. "Call Gil!" she commanded Hudson, and leaned her weight against the big portal window while the Highrise manager slammed his palms against the glass and cried (muffled though it was), "Let me out! Let me out!"

Having both a cell phone and the presence of mind not to argue with a woman whom he'd just discovered possessed not only the vim but also the vigor to lock a grown man inside a clothes dryer, Hudson dialed the number. And when the call was answered with a hopeful "Is there news?" instead of the stoic "Gil Borsch here," Hudson felt almost guilty about the news he did have. "No," he replied, then quickly added, "Any chance you could get to the Senior Highrise? Rita's trapped Vince Garnucci in a dryer. Looks like he's the Nightie-Napper."

"She's . . . wait . . . *what*?"

"You heard me, Gil."

After a short hesitation, the lawman said, "That sounds like something *Sammy* would do."

Hudson frowned as he eyed his wife, wedged up against the dryer. "Must be the shoes."

"What's that?"

"Can you just get here? We're in the basement. I don't know how long a man can breathe inside a closed dryer."

"On my way," Gil said, and clicked off.

Inside the dryer, Vince Garnucci had collapsed into a wretched puddle of pleas. And although the pleas themselves were not quite discernible through the glass (or the tears), it was clear that the man was losing it.

"Let him out, Rita. He's harmless."

"He's a thief!" Rita countered.

Hudson nodded. "Let him out."

Rita turned and studied the manager through the glass, then opened the door ever so slightly. "Confess," she said through the crack. "Or get tumbled!"

What came through the opening was a long, gasp-riddled barrage of incoherent (and very weepy) verbiage. And when the manager collapsed back into a balled-up position at the bottom of the dryer, Hudson asked, "What did he say?"

Rita shook her head. "Something about his grandmother being demanding and unreasonable."

Hudson Graham had an exquisite opportunity to make a joke at Rita's expense, but instead simply said, "Rita, the man's in obvious pain. I don't know how long he can breathe in there, and we're not going to tumble a confession out of him. Let him out."

So Rita relented.

Which Hudson immediately regretted.

With the eyes of a madman (or maybe just those of a man trapped in a dryer by a madwoman in high-tops), Vince Garnucci darted out of the laundry room, neatly avoiding Hudson with a quick zig and a long zag around a row of washers.

And while Hudson was calling, "Mr. Garnucci! It does no good to run away!" Rita was zigging around him in hot pursuit. "Rita!" the septuagenarian called after her, but that, too, was to no avail. Rita simply shouted, "He's the *Nightie-Napper*!" like it was a crime of unparalleled proportions (while also clearly conveying that Hudson had better get his boots in gear to help her undo the damage he'd caused).

Unfortunately for Hudson, he was not familiar with the labyrinth of basement hallways, doorways, and shortcuts.

Also unfortunate for Hudson was that he couldn't track his bride by the *ticky-tap-tapp*ing of her shoes as he normally might.

There was also the dilemma of having told Gil Borsch that they were in the Highrise basement—something he felt he should update the lawman about as soon as possible.

This collective of unfortunates was, however, nothing in relation to the huge unfortunate of having given his new wife advice that had backfired.

Still. It was with great relief that Hudson wound up on the first floor and immediately heard his wife's voice (shouting as it was) from down a hallway near the manager's desk. This was followed almost immediately by the additional relief of Sergeant Borsch whooshing in through the front door.

"Gil!" Hudson called. "This way!"

So the two men raced toward the sound of Rita's voice and skidded to a halt when they saw Rita with her foot jammed in a doorway, preventing an apartment door with a dull brass MANAGER plaque on it from closing. "This is not a joke, Vince!" she was shouting. "And I'm not dropping it!"

"*How* old is she?" Gil asked, forgetting his manners (which were notoriously MIA anyway) as he took in the scene.

Hudson shook his head and neatly avoided the question. "I tell you, it's the shoes."

"Rita," Sergeant Borsch said, approaching the impasse. "Let me handle it."

"Hrmph!" Rita said. "If by 'handle it' you mean you're going to let him get away again, no thank you! This building has been terrorized by the Nightie-Napper for . . . for years!"

"Terrorized?" Gil said with a bit of a smirk. "By someone who steals nightgowns?"

"It's not just nightgowns! And don't you mock me, Gilbert Borsch! Ask anyone who lives here—the situation has been very unsettling!"

Now, there is clearly a huge gap between being unsettled and being terrorized, but Gil Borsch (wisely) didn't make an issue of it. Instead, he calmly reached over Rita's shoulder and knocked on the door. "Police!" he barked. "Give yourself up, Garnucci."

And just like that, the pressure Vince Garnucci had been exerting on the inside of the apartment door ceased, causing the outside pressure Rita had been exerting to fling the door open.

Hudson had been to the Highrise enough to have had many friendly exchanges with Vince Garnucci. Usually the topic was the weather, but one time the manager had told him a long story about his grandmother's foray into a seedier side of town, where she'd been on her bicycle in search of some organic agave for her afternoon tea. "I guess I was too slow finding some for her, so she set out to do it herself," the manager had said with a laugh. "I will never hear the end of it!"

Hudson had mentioned the exchange to Rita, who had advised him to avoid conversations concerning the grandmother at all costs. "Once he starts," she'd warned him, "he goes on and on and on and on!"

And that had been the extent of the thought Hudson had given to Vince Garnucci's bicycle-riding grandmother. Only now as the man disappeared down a hallway inside the apartment (leaving his front door wide open) did Hudson realize there was something peculiar about the situation. (Well, beyond a grown man stealing old ladies' nightgowns, that is.) "Does his grandmother live here?" he whispered to Rita.

"I've never seen her," Rita whispered back. "I was under the impression that she lived across town."

But the question was understandable because the apartment was furnished in florals. From the slipcovers on the couch, to the window treatments, to the kitchen-chair cushions, to the lampshades, the place was like a three-dimensional quilt of unmatched flowery fabrics.

And then to the left, partly tucked away behind the

door, Hudson noticed a bicycle. An old-fashioned, one-speed, yellow, slant-framed bicycle with a white basket (adorned with synthetic flowers), faded blue-and-yellow handle ribbons, and a classic *ching-ching* handlebar bell.

"Something's not right here," Hudson said, to which Gil Borsch muttered, "You can say that again."

Then Rita (referring to the abundance of overlapping pillows propped neatly along the back of the couch) whispered, "I believe those used to be Rose Wedgewood's muumuu."

"I mean, beyond theft," Hudson said, pointing out the bicycle. "Something's not right here."

"Oh!" Rita gasped. "She *does* live here?"

Wanting to get a better look, Rita stepped over the threshold, but both Hudson and Sergeant Borsch pulled her back. "We don't want to compromise the investigation with an unlawful entry," Hudson said.

"Exactly!" Sergeant Borsch agreed, eyeing Hudson with appreciation. Then he cupped his mouth and bellowed, "Garnucci! Get out here!"

From inside the apartment, a gray-haired woman appeared. She was wearing glasses, a collared floral dress, and Velcro-close shoes, and was relying heavily on a cane. "Go away," came her high, warbly voice. "I'll pay for the damages. Vinnie has been through enough."

The trio stared at the woman a moment, not wanting to argue with her. She was, after all, *old*. Far older than Hudson or Rita.

But Sergeant Borsch eventually managed to clear his throat and say, "I'm sorry, ma'am, but—"

"I said I'd pay!" she warbled, taking another step forward.

And that was when Hudson noticed something peculiar. "Uh, Gil," he whispered as he leaned over to speak to the lawman. "Look at the arms."

"Huh?" Gil asked.

"The *hair* on the arms? It's brown. And rather thick?"

With a jolt of horror Sergeant Borsch and Rita simultaneously realized what Hudson had already concluded: This woman was neither old nor (actually) a woman.

"I'm feeling very *Psycho*," Gil Borsch said under his breath. "Rita, you might want to back up."

"Vince," Hudson said calmly to the (wigged-out) man, "we know that's you."

"I am *Carlotta*," came the high (not-quite-so-warbly) voice. "And I demand that you leave us alone!"

"Sorry," Sergeant Borsch informed him. "Not gonna happen."

From the bits and pieces Vince Garnucci had relayed about his grandmother, it should have been pretty clear to the others that she was a woman who didn't take no for an answer, and this version of Carlotta Garnucci was certainly living up to that reputation. Rather than surrender or retreat, she attacked.

Fortunately, she was not a knife-wielding psycho, but simply a bike-bashing one. In a flash, the fake, flowered female was behind the fake-flowered basket, ramming the bicycle (wheel first) out the door and into Sergeant Borsch.

"That's it," the Borschman said, and in a surprisingly agile series of moves (and despite the still-present kink in

111

his neck) he had the Highrise manager on the floor and securely handcuffed. "Looks like this one's going to the psych ward," he muttered. And after he'd radioed the station and had had a moment to catch his breath, he eyed Rita's feet and said, "I need you to go home and change your shoes."

Rita gave him a puzzled look, but Hudson threw back his head and laughed. Then he put his arm around Rita and pulled her along, saying, "Sammy's going to love hearing all about this."

And that's when the realization of the situation returned to Rita full force.

Vince Garnucci (and his bicycle-riding grandma) had been an effective distraction, but it was time to get back to the hospital.

Back to Sammy.

13—RIBBONS

Back at the hospital, of all the people congregating in the ICU waiting room (or squealing behind the nurses' station), the only one who knew Darren or Lana or Marko personally was Marissa, and she knew all three.

Casey and Heather had *met* all three.

In Las Vegas.

Briefly.

And Casey had *heard* about all three in great (sometimes disgruntled, sometimes humorous) detail from Sammy.

But Casey and Heather were not people to whom Marko would entrust seventeen teddy bears (and a rogue unicorn).

Marissa, however, was.

"Oh, that's a great idea!" she cried when Marko had explained the plan. Then she set about passing around bears and Sharpies and instructions to all assembled, before fetching scissors from the nurses' station so she could issue every bear a length of ribbon.

"Good choice," Darren told Marko about Marissa, then led the drummer (and Lana) down the hallway to

Room 411, leaving starstruck hospital personnel in their wake.

Zelda Quinn had instructed her cameraman to capture some B-roll footage of Darren Cole because an interview had clearly been out of the question at that juncture. What with the bald guy and the teddy bears and all.

But after the two Troublemakers and the diva had left the waiting room, the cameraman came out from behind his equipment with wide eyes and gasped, "That was Marko Rushmore!"

"Who?" Zelda asked, and her eyes narrowed suspiciously at the cameraman's uncharacteristic enthusiasm.

"Marko Rushmore!" he said. "The Troublemakers' drummer?"

Now, being a front-and-center performer herself, Zelda Quinn did not know (or care) who anyone besides the lead singer in the band was. And if *she* didn't know (or care) who the drummer was, nobody in her viewing audience would know (or care) who he was, either.

"Tell me you didn't shoot him instead of Darren Cole," she said.

"You're kidding, right?" the cameraman replied. "You'd rather get footage of a guy standing by than one delivering *teddy bears* to kids?"

"When the guy standing by is Darren Cole, yes!" she seethed. "When I tell you to cover the guy standing by, *yes*."

"But look at them!" the cameraman said, pointing to the remaining crowd. "You don't think *that's* a story?"

"It's *my* job to say what's a story," she snapped. "It's *your* job to shoot that story!"

But then she turned and saw the scene without the presence of Darren Cole blinding her. Those kids she'd talked to earlier and the oddball adults were huddled in waiting-room chairs or sitting cross-legged on the floor, intently writing messages on ribbons.

And teddy bears were everywhere.

It was actually a very moving scene.

"Keep in mind they're minors," she warned her photographer (conceding his point without actually admitting it, while simultaneously reminding him to shoot in such a way as to avoid faces). Then she wandered back out into the main room.

After observing the quiet activity for several minutes, Zelda sat (somewhat awkwardly) on the floor alongside Billy Pratt. "May I?" she asked, then eased the ribbon from him and began reading aloud. "Zombies to the Rescue! Graveyard Golf Cart! Grim and Reaper! Laddies Gone Amok! The Black Pearl! Bucket o' Bones! Condor Rescue! Not a 5-Person Tent! Drool Monster!"

Then, as if there was a delay to her brain in registering what her mouth was saying, she suddenly backed up on the ribbon, saying, "Wait. 'Condor Rescue'?" She looked at Billy. "Were *you* the kids who rescued that condor last summer?"

"Du-uh" might have been a suitable response, but Billy simply nodded. "Me and Sammy and him," he said, pointing over to Casey, "and . . ." He looked around and called out, "Hey, Cricket should be here."

"I have her number," Dot volunteered, and interrupted her own ribbon writing to call her.

Now, Zelda Quinn's interest in the condor story had nothing whatsoever to do with condors. Zelda Quinn's interest in the condor story had to do with how it had gotten her rival, Grayson Mann, fired.

And these kids had been the ones who had brought him down?

She stared at Billy as the full weight of his words landed. "So . . . you and him," she said, pointing to Casey, "and your friend who's in a coma . . . you're the ones who put Grayson Mann in jail?"

"Well, mostly Sammy did," Billy said, taking the ribbon back. "Sammy and Cricket and Casey."

The gratitude she felt made Zelda oddly uncomfortable. Almost vulnerable. And not knowing how to handle these emotions, she turned to Dot (who had left Cricket a message and was sitting nearby) and said, "So what have you written?"

Dot held up her ribbon and read, "Fire! Fire!" and "The Monster from the Marsh!" but was interrupted by an excited Marissa, who exclaimed, "That was Halloween! Seventh grade! The Bush House!" (She was not, as you might reasonably conclude, reading from her own ribbon, but rather reacting to Dot's.)

"Right!" Dot laughed. "Remember your mummy costume?"

"Don't remind me!" Marissa laughed. Then she pointed at Dot's ribbon and said, "What else do you have?"

So Dot continued reading. "Nibbles Swallowed the Key!"

"Who's Nibbles?" Zelda asked.

"Dot's crazy dog!" cried a chorus of teen voices.

Dot laughed and went on. "Ghosts in the Carriage House! Penny the Pig!"

"That was New Year's of seventh grade!" Marissa cried. "When we found that meth lab!"

"A meth lab?" Zelda asked, her head whipping back and forth between Dot and Marissa. "Are you talking about that one out in Sisquane? That was *you*?"

"It was *gnarly*," Marissa said, but Dot was already back to the ribbon. "Lucky Thirteen! Kickstart Her Broom!"

"Hey!" Heather snapped (because this was a reference to her, and she remembered the sting of the quip when Sammy had originally delivered it). "Not nice!"

Dot blushed but went on. "Water Hoops! Pepernoten! Land of Blue Invasion!" She looked up and smiled. "That's it."

So Marissa took over, reading her ribbon. "I've got . . . Double Dynamos! Elvis! Timber! Hollywood! Renaissance Faire! Loopy Noogies! Deli-Mustard Car!"

"The deli-mustard car!" Billy and Casey and Holly all cried, remembering how they'd narrowly escaped being trapped in the graveyard on Halloween.

"Paper Trail!" Marissa continued. "Employees Only Doors! Roof of the Mall! Awesome Dome of Dryness!"

Marissa looked up, so Holly took over, calling out, "Psycho Kitties! Canine Calendar Float! Catcher's Mitt! Smackdown at the Mall!"

"HEY!" Heather shouted. "That's . . . not . . . nice!" (Because she had, in fact, been the one smacked down.)

But over her shoulder, Holly snarled, "Like you've *ever* been nice to me?"

"What have I done to you?"

The waiting room fell quiet as Holly's head turned like the turret of a tank to face her. And as Heather gulped, Holly fired. "Do the names Trash Digger and Homeless Hag and Ugly Orphan ring any bells?"

Heather gave a little cringe, then tried, "Sticks and stones . . . ?" But then she remembered something that revived her. "And speaking of stones . . . you *slugged* me in the stomach, remember that?"

"Because you ambushed Sammy!" Holly snapped. "Remember *that*?"

"Stop it!" Casey said. "This isn't helping anything. We're supposed to be doing something positive here, not beating each other up. Heather's trying to be a better person. So help her out instead of sniping at her."

Holly heaved a sigh and turned her back on Heather again, but Heather (who'd only managed to come up with Backstage Passes! and House of Blues! for her ribbon) said, "Doesn't anyone want to come up with a list of people who Sammy's gotten arrested? People who might want revenge?"

"That," Justice Jack announced from where he was hanging with the other oddball adults, "is a brilliant idea!" He stepped forward with the index finger of a Golden Glove of Justice raised. "I *told* her she should wear a mask!"

"A *mask*?" Heather said with a nasty squint, but then immediately dialed back the attitude. "Look, can we just deal with the here and now? Who could have done this to her?"

"What about those counterfeiters?" Marissa said. "What happened to them?"

Billy nodded. "Or what about that crazy lady who buried her husband in the backyard?"

"Or that creep with the meth lab?" Casey said. "Whatever happened to him?"

"Or that gang guy?" Marissa said with a shudder. "I know he got locked up, but is he still locked up?"

Madame Nashira stepped forward. "She also busted that crook who broke into my room and stole from me."

"I remember him," André growled through his cigar stub. "And what about Shovel Man?" He looked at Holly. "What was his real name?"

Holly shook her head. "He wasn't—"

But her answer was cut short by Slammin' Dave, who threw in, "What about those guys with the cat-fighting ring? Are they serving time?"

"Or the world's worst teacher!" Billy cried. "The whole 'Die, dude!' thing?"

"But he didn't go to jail," Casey said.

"Still, he hates Sammy. She got him fired!"

Casey nodded. "So true."

"Or . . . ," Holly said, "how about that lady who was blackmailing everyone in town? What happened to her?"

"Or the guy who almost murdered the Bush Man?" Dot cried. "Where's he?"

Zelda Quinn shook her head as if trying to clear her

hearing. "Are you saying Sammy was involved in *all* of those?"

"Yes!" came a collective cry.

"Which is why we should stop waiting for Sergeant Borsch and write them down ourselves!" Heather said. "We need to be systematic! Eliminate possibilities! Figure out who had motive and who had opportunity!"

The rest of the teens stared at her.

"Motive and opportunity?" Marissa asked with a little squint.

"Yes!"

Marissa's squint grew deeper. "Who *are* you?"

Everyone stared until Billy Pratt broke the silence. "Heather's right. We should get on it."

So after everyone agreed (some more grudgingly than others), Zelda turned to her phone and started making calls. She had no idea whether Grayson Mann was still serving time for his role in the condor caper, but if he was out, she'd be sure to have the kids put his name at the top of their list.

14—THE DECISION

Inside Room 411, Marko was dominating the conversation. (Or, more precisely, the monologue.) "You're the Samminator!" he was saying. "You can't take this lying down! You need to fight back! Rumor is you've got a smashin' right hook, so come on! I want to see it in action!" Then, like a trucker grinding into a downshift, he switched gears. "Besides, you've got to get up and give your uncle Marko a hug! And you've got to see what's going on in the waiting room. The place is full of people! And teddy bears!" Then, in a very mysterious tone, he started singing a song his mother had sung to him as a child:

> *"If you go down to the woods today, you're sure of a
>   big surprise.*
> *If you go down to the woods today, you'd better go in
>   disguise!*
> *For every bear that ever-there-was will gather there
>   for certain because . . .*
> *Today's the day the teddy bears have their
>   picnic. . . ."*

While Marko talked and sang, and Lana silently held her daughter's hand, Darren sat in the far corner, first rubbing the little horseshoe that was laced onto one of Sammy's shoes, then slowly turning the high-top in his hands, trying to commit to memory all the words and sketches Casey had inked into the fabric. He had missed out bigtime, but holding the shoes, reading the shoes, somehow made him feel better. He could almost imagine the adventures Sammy had been on. All the excitement.

Maybe it was the exclamation points.

He turned the shoe some more, mentally erasing the punctuation. He'd been instructed as a student to avoid excessive or superfluous punctuation. Especially exclamation points. But now he wondered why that was. Was it so wrong to be excited? Was it wrong to be joyful? Was it wrong to feel *alive*?

Lost in thought, Darren hadn't noticed that Marko had gone silent. Or that his best friend was fighting back tears of his own. But now that he *did* notice, he realized that he had never seen the drummer cry before. Well, there was the time when they were eight and Marko had totaled his new bicycle in one wicked miscalculation of speed and distance, but Marko's tears then had been more for the destruction of the bike than the blood and skin he'd left smeared along the asphalt. No, Marko had always been . . . rugged. Even when skinned to a bloody pulp.

So Darren was trying to figure out what to say when someone from the medical staff entered the room.

"Oh!" the man said, and seemed taken aback by all the visitors in the room. He glanced over his shoulder, then said, "I'm sorry, but you're going to have to leave until after we run a few tests."

Darren stood, carefully putting the shoes aside. "Let's go," he told the others.

But Lana turned to the med guy and said, "Are you running the tests in here?"

The man nodded.

"What sort of tests?" she asked.

The man tried to conceal his impatience as he indicated the equipment obstructed by Lana. "I'm just here to prep the machinery, ma'am. Now, if you don't mind . . . ?"

Not wanting to contribute to the delay or obstruction of any tests that might get to the bottom of Sammy's condition, Darren and Marko were already moving toward the door.

But Lana (who didn't take kindly to being ma'am-ed instead of miss-ed, *especially* by someone clearly older than she was) revived her inner diva. "What machinery?" Then she eyed his worn shoes, white socks, and high-water scrubs. "Are *you* the technician?"

"No, ma'am. I'm the prep guy. Now, if you'll—"

"The prep guy," she said with a disapproving frown. "What's a prep guy?"

"Look, I'll come back," he said, and beat a swift exit from the room.

"Lana . . ." Darren sighed. "He was just trying to do his job." Then he started after the man, who was already out the door.

"What kind of hospital lets their personnel dress that way?" Lana called over her shoulder. "His greens even clash!" she cried, referring to the mismatched hues of his scrubs.

Once outside Room 411, Darren looked left, then right, for the mismatched prep guy. And since to the right was basically a dead end, he went left, toward the nurses' station.

Midway down the hall he came upon Nurse Faith (the one with the guitar smock), who had been hoping to catch another glimpse of the rock star. And to her heart-strumming delight, she got more than just a glimpse. Darren Cole looked directly at her and spoke. "Did the prep guy come this way?"

"The *prep* guy?" she asked, as if trying to adapt to some new, cool rocker slang.

"He was just in my daughter's room. To set up for some tests?"

"Tests?" she asked. And it appeared that the poor woman was starstruck beyond competence, only then she said, "I don't believe any tests have been ordered."

Darren's head quivered impatiently. "He said he was there to prep the machinery."

"Prep the machinery?"

"Yes. For tests."

"Well, come with me," she said, and led him to the nurses' station, where she checked charts and records (both physical and electronic), then asked the other personnel inside the station if they had any knowledge of tests having been ordered, or to whom this (clearly stressed) father might be referring as "the prep guy."

"Sorry," Nurse Faith said when she'd collected enough

head shakes and shrugs. "There's been no order for additional tests."

"Are you *sure*?"

The nurse nodded.

"So who was that man in the room?" the rocker asked.

"Well . . . what did he look like?"

"Brown hair. Glasses. About forty?" Then with a little frown he conceded, "I'm not the best with ages."

"Maybe Vick?" one of the nurses behind the counter volunteered.

"Or Steve?" another suggested.

"Could have been Ian? I think it's his shift."

Darren hesitated. Obviously, a better description was needed. He didn't want to insult the staff, but something about the left hand not knowing what the right hand was doing *was* bothering him. So he finally just came out with it. "He wasn't put together very well."

"Put together?" Nurse Faith asked, clearly envisioning robotics or a Frankenstein monster.

"His scrubs didn't match. And they were high-waters. And his shoes were dingy."

A woman inside the nurses' station laughed. "Could be Vick, Steve, *or* Ian!"

It appeared to Darren that he'd reached a dead end, which both irritated and confused him. How could they not know who'd been sent to the room? And more importantly, how could they not know *why* he'd been sent?

"Dr. Jha will be here soon," Nurse Six-strings offered. "I'm sure he'll be able to clear this up."

Just then Marko came up and said, "Lana says she's not

125

leaving Sammy's side. That they'll just have to do the tests with her there." Then he picked up on the tension and asked, "What's going on?"

So Darren took him aside and was in the middle of letting off some controlled steam about what was *not* going on when Zelda Quinn approached.

"Excuse me," she said.

Darren turned, and even though the woman had no telltale paraphernalia (like, say, a microphone or a logoed ball cap or a station polo shirt), in the blink of an eye he recognized her for what she was.

A reporter.

The last thing Darren wanted to deal with at the moment was a reporter. But then Marko said, "I like the do" (in reference to Zelda's unique hairstyle), and suddenly a man in beige walking shorts was upon them, extending his hand toward Marko, saying, "Sorry about the circumstances, but I've just got to tell you—I'm such a fan!"

"Alton!" Zelda snapped, but Marko took it in stride. "You play?" he asked as he clasped the man's hand and noted his well-defined calf muscles.

"My whole life," the cameraman said in a gust of awe.

Zelda gave Alton a dark look, then turned to Darren and said, "Please excuse my overzealous cameraman. We don't mean to intrude on your privacy; we're just hoping to help. Your daughter is obviously a very special person, and after talking to her friends here, I understand that she's also a hometown hero. I don't want to exploit her, or you, or the situation for that matter, but if there was ever a time when your celebrity could be put to good use, it's now."

Darren studied her a moment, wondering if this was just a clever butter-up. Was her calling an exploit an exploit merely a tricky way of getting him to agree to be exploited?

He had his suspicions, but still, there's nothing like a person complimenting your child to predispose you to liking them.

And the cameraman being a fan of Marko's didn't hurt, either.

Actually, it kind of helped. At least it wasn't a typical rush-and-gush where the feasting was on him while his bandmate was tossed a few scraps, at best.

So at last he said, "Go on."

Zelda took an urgent step forward. "I can't help with the medical side of things, but I *can* get the community behind tracking down who did this." She locked eyes with him. "I had planned to make the plea myself, but people would sit up and listen—actually rewind in their minds and *think*—if the plea came from you."

Darren studied her a moment, then glanced over at Marko, who gave him a rapid head shake.

Zelda (who caught the shake-shake) lowered her voice and said, "The more time that passes, the less chance we'll have of catching the guy. If we're going to get this out on the five and the six, I've got to get moving." She watched the gears turn in Darren's mind for a moment, then tried to close the deal. "I know how to put together a sensitive story. I really just want to help."

Again Darren glanced at Marko, who responded with a huddle-up-bro head jerk.

127

"Excuse me for a minute," Darren told the reporter, then gave the drummer a little sideways head jerk of his own, signaling him to confer with him in an empty corner.

"Dude, she's working you," Marko whispered when their heads were together. "Do what she wants and this place will be full of people angling for a piece of you."

"I think it might help to find the guy," Darren whispered. "Somebody's got to know something."

"Look. Find out what the cops have first."

"We would have heard if they had anything. And she's under deadline."

"Of course she is," Marko growled. Then he added, "And how's Lana gonna like it, huh? When the place is crawlin' with chicks?"

"It's not going to be crawling with chicks."

"Well, dames, then. Dames for sure."

Darren frowned at his friend's attempt at humor. "Knock it off, Marko."

"Fine. Sorry. But look. They're not allowed to ID a minor without a parent's consent. You do this and everything becomes fair game."

"But I think it might help," Darren said again, picking anxiously at the callus on the tip of his ring finger. "And the hospital won't let things get out of control."

"Things are already out of control!"

"It'll be fine."

Marko frowned, then eyed the reporter over Darren's shoulder. "Here she comes, dude. And I take it back about the hair. I think I smell a polecat."

"I'm sorry," Zelda said, giving Darren a concerned look, "but we are running out of time."

Darren nodded, bit his lip, nodded again, and then (since nothing felt worse than idle helplessness) he nodded for real. "Let's do it."

15—BILLY

While Darren was off in one corner of the waiting room, huddled with Marko, deciding not to confer with the cops before making a public plea, Casey was in another corner, on the phone, trying to reach Sergeant Borsch.

"Well?" Marissa asked after he'd clicked off.

"They told me he's unavailable because he's processing an arrest."

"An arrest?" Marissa gasped. "Was it the guy?"

"She wouldn't say."

"But . . . it could be?" Marissa asked.

"It could be anybody," Heather grumbled.

"Including the guy who did this to Sammy!" Marissa snarled.

Heather shook her head. "We should still make the list."

"But if the guy's been arrested—"

"We don't *know* that," Heather snapped. "And what are the chances? This is Santa Martina, remember? Not Disneyland. Besides, it'd be nothing to write down the things you were just talking about."

There was a moment of tense silence, and then Dot

sighed and said, "Isn't anyone else starving? It's almost three o'clock and I haven't had a bite since breakfast."

If there's one thing that can make a group of teenagers agree on a course of action, it's hunger. Just like that, all six teens decided that the food court in the mall would be a much better place to make their list of revenge-minded criminals than the waiting room of the ICU.

Especially since the ICU staff was now telling them to pick up all their "craft stuff."

And that bears couldn't occupy waiting-room chairs.

The place was starting to feel a little too much like school (especially since Ms. Rothhammer had just been joined by Mr. Tiller and Mrs. Ambler and their vice principal from last year, Mr. Caan). And since the mall wasn't far to walk *and* happened to be very near the police station (with food-court offerings much more to their taste than those of the hospital's cafeteria), they picked up their stuff, slung on their backpacks, returned their ribbon-wrapped bears to Marko, and went to the mall.

And while food-court fare was being consumed and drinks were being refilled and other people from school (including Cricket) were joining the group and exchanging what they knew about "the Sammy situation," Heather kept quiet, looking across the table at Marissa from time to time, only to get visually slapped by Marissa's fierce glares.

Heather considered that this flare-up of anger might have something to do with her fling with Danny Urbanski, since they were near the location of a showdown that had involved him. But Marissa seemed to be done with him—and so, for that matter, was she—so that wasn't it.

And it could have been all the stuff she'd pulled on Marissa and Sammy in the past, but she'd apologized to both of them and had really been trying to make amends. And although she knew she'd never live down all the things she'd done, she'd been diligently following her counselor's advice to proceed slowly and avoid backslides.

Which wasn't easy.

Especially when people treated her like a pariah.

So Marissa's glares *could* have been for any number of things, but the increased hostility was showing up now. At the food court. Very near where she'd called Marissa's pudgy little brother Blubber Boy for the whole after-school crowd to hear. It had been a quick, off-the-cuff jab, and when Sammy had challenged her, pointing out that the kid had feelings, she'd made some remark about not being able to see his feelings, buried under all his fat.

And as Heather sat there, ignored (except for the occasional glare) and feeling like an outcast, a little voice inside her head told her that she'd been right.

The kid *was* fat.

What she'd said *had* been funny.

The little voice brought a certain level of comfort. A kind of relief from the pressures of change. And with that comfort, a snarl began forming at Heather's lip. She didn't deserve to be treated like a pariah! Not after how hard she'd been trying to make up for the past. If Sammy died (or was in a coma forever), did she want to be friends with these people? With Marissa and Holly and goody-goody-Dutch-shoes *Dot*?

"You okay?" came a voice in her ear.

She started, then turned.

It was Casey.

"No," she told him, and suddenly she felt like crying. "I don't think I want to be here."

"Why aren't we making that list?" he said, noticing the blank piece of paper in front of her and the Sharpie in her hand. Then he turned to the others and called, "Hey! Hey, guys! Let's get going on the list!"

When everyone had moved closer, Heather passed the paper and the marker over to Marissa. "Here. You should do this."

When a long-standing enemy offers an olive branch, it's not always easy to take it. But although the two girls locked eyes for a long (somewhat tense) moment, and although Marissa would have been (mostly) justified in saying, Darned right I should! she finally just gave a silent nod of thanks and accepted the paper and pen.

"Okay," Marissa said, "let's start with that hotel thief."

"The guy Sammy waved at?" Dot asked. "I heard about that! She was using binoculars and spotted him stealing stuff. And when he looked up and saw her, she waved at him!"

"That's the one!" Marissa said, and everyone laughed.

So Marissa started jotting things down, sketching a rough chart of people, from politicians Sammy had thwarted to criminals she'd trapped, writing as quickly (and still legibly) as she could while people threw in names and rumors they'd heard and remember-whens.

And with each new story shared, the crowd around the original group grew.

As did the embellishment of each story.

Then all eyes turned to Billy, who took the stage and reminded everyone about his stint as Justice Jack's sidekick and how they had helped Sammy restore law and order (and City Hall's infamous softball statue). But suddenly, mid-sentence, Billy stopped talking, and his face (which had been flushed and alive the moment before) went pale and slack.

"Billy?" Dot asked with a concerned quiver in her voice. But then she turned to look where Billy (and now everybody else) was staring.

"Uh-oh," Casey said as a group of students parted to let a man approach. He was obviously angry and had (at least) a three-day stubble.

"Who is that?" Heather whispered.

Casey (being the only one besides Billy who knew) answered. "That's Billy's dad."

When Mr. Pratt was within striking distance of his son, he growled, "I told you what you were in for if you ditched again." And Billy (who was stuck between mortified and terrified) tried to explain. "My friend was—"

"Don't *start* that crap with me!" Mr. Pratt shouted as he grabbed his son by the arm. "Get home! Now!"

Billy's father was not particularly tall. Or particularly large. But he had an ominous presence, and as he man-handled his son forward, Billy's friends gave them wide berth.

For Mr. Pratt, however, it wasn't wide enough. "What are you kids starin' at?" he shouted. "Mind your own damn business!"

The little hints Billy had dropped about his father

suddenly congealed into what seemed like a monster rearing up from a dark, bubbling pool. And as the stunned teens watched Billy get dragged away, no one seemed to know what to do, or how to help.

Dot gasped, "Billy shouldn't be in trouble for *caring*."

"There's no talking to his dad when he's like this," Casey said. "It just makes things worse."

"It looks pretty bad right now!" Marissa cried.

Dot turned to Casey. "Does Billy's dad hit him? Because it sure looks like that's what he's planning to do."

Casey (who'd been sworn to secrecy by Billy) looked away.

"We can't just let him beat Billy up!" Dot cried. "We have to *do* something!" Then she looked around and said, "*Sammy* wouldn't let him beat Billy up!"

"That's right," Marissa said. "She'd clonk him over the head with her skateboard!"

"Or cement him in a wheelbarrow!"

"Or run him down with a motor home!"

Heather frowned. "Don't you guys ever just call 911?"

"And say what?" Casey asked. " 'My friend's dad hauled him home for ditching school'?"

"That's right," someone in the crowd volunteered. "They won't do anything until *after* he's beat up."

Casey nodded. "And Billy's never gonna cop to it."

"He'll just take his lickin' and keep on tickin'!" another guy called.

"This is *not* funny!" Dot cried. "We need to *do* something!" She turned to Casey. "Where does he live? We have to go over there and *do* something."

Casey frowned. He'd seen Billy's dad in a rage before, but he'd never actually seen him hit Billy. And he'd always gone along with Billy's insistence that "Ma pappy's just a hurricane running its course. You hold on, and then it's over."

Billy never talked about the damage.

Or the things that were impossible to repair.

But for all the hiding and covering up Billy did, Casey knew Dot was right—if Sammy were there, she would *do* something. It would likely get them into trouble, or danger (and this was definitely a *sidetrack* from what they'd set out to do), but Sammy wouldn't just sit around the mall wondering what was happening to her friend.

So he eyed Dot and said, "You think we should storm the castle, huh?"

"Yes!" she cried.

"Uh-oh," Marissa said, because she knew exactly what that meant.

"You guys are nuts," Heather grumbled, but she was the first one to swing on her backpack.

In all, only six of the teens went to "storm the castle"— the original five plus Cricket. And on the way over, Cricket (keeping her voice low because she, too, was uncertain about the New Heather) told Dot, "Thank you so much for calling me. I'm really, really glad I'm here." Then she gave Dot a shy look and said, "I always want to do stuff with you guys, but . . . it's usually over before I hear about it."

Dot nodded. "I feel that way sometimes." She smiled at Cricket. "I'm not usually the one who wants to storm the castle." And then, because she had a pretty good idea what Cricket was feeling, she added, "Sammy really likes you, Cricket. She still talks about that camping trip you guys took."

Cricket gave her a grateful smile and nodded. "That trip was crazy." Then she added, "We ran into Billy out in the wilderness. He was so funny."

"Yeah?"

"He had this huge rattlesnake."

"Billy did?"

Cricket nodded. "It was dead and he was carrying it like a jump rope and being so crazy with it that I told him he should chop the head off before he injected himself with venom. So he laughed and told the snake, 'Time for the guillotine, serpentine!'"

"That is so Billy," Dot laughed.

"Isn't it?" Cricket said, then shook her head a little and sighed, "I just love Billy."

"Me, too," Dot said with a sigh of her own.

Then both girls (suddenly realizing the real emotion behind what the other had said) looked at each other with wide eyes and, without a word, put up pinky fingers, linked them silently together, and smiled.

"What are you two doing?" Marissa asked.

Cricket and Dot (both recalling how Marissa had insanely dumped Billy for the lying, cheating Danny Urbanski) chimed, "Nothing."

Marissa might have pressed them, but just then Casey turned onto an apartment-complex walkway, and the pinky swear she'd witnessed completely vanished from her mind. "He lives *here*?" she gasped as they walked along, because the buildings weren't just badly maintained, they had an ominous shadowiness to them. Like the sun was not welcome and any respectable breeze would think twice before blowing in.

"You never visited him?" Cricket asked Marissa. "You know, when you were going out?"

Marissa shook her head. "He always wanted to meet somewhere." Her voice was low, almost a whisper. "Now I understand why."

Casey led the group along the walkway toward a back corner of the complex. As they approached, it became clear which apartment was Billy's, not from a sign on the door announcing PRATT FAMILY, but from the sounds coming through it.

"Oh, no!" Marissa cried, because both the volume and the language were extreme, and they weren't even at the apartment yet. And after hearing what Mr. Pratt was yelling at his son, Dot's eyes welled with tears and she asked, "How can he say those things to him?"

"That is definitely abuse," Holly said. "I wish we had a recorder!"

"We do," Heather said, and took out her phone.

Cricket gasped, "Of course! Great idea!" and Heather gave her a quick, grateful smile.

Casey had approached the apartment window, which was past the front door and in the shadows. The curtain was not drawn, and after getting a look inside, Casey signaled his sister to get over to him fast.

Heather had a reputation for being sneaky, calculating, and vindictive. She was also known for being gutsy and brash—someone who could pull off stunts others wouldn't dream of trying. So sneaking up to a window to record what was going on inside was nothing compared to other things she'd done, and yet her hands wouldn't stay steady as she videoed the scene inside the apartment. And after only ten seconds she could no longer put gathering proof above stopping Billy's dad from beating up his son. "Stop it!" she screamed, knocking on the window. "Stop hitting him!"

The apartment fell quiet.

The curtain flew closed.

And then the six teens stood terrified, sure that the door was about to fly open and the Monster would turn his rage on them.

But it did not.

And *he* did not.

And as the silence continued, Heather (with shaky hands and a pounding heart) showed the others the footage she'd managed to capture on her phone.

"He's just going to hit him harder after we leave," Holly whispered.

Dot nodded. "What's to stop him?"

"Us," Marissa said, then looked right at Heather. "You were right."

"I was?" Heather said.

Marissa nodded. "We need to call 911."

16—BLACKMAIL

It had taken longer than expected to get the Nightie-Napper tucked safely away in jail, and Gil Borsch had just finished documenting the Garnucci Incident when something in the quiet radio traffic at his side caught his attention.

Recognizing the address being relayed, he turned up the volume, and when the apartment number was specified and he heard the description of a "frantic group of teens," he was up in a flash, certain that the teens were Sammy's troupe (with the absence, of course, of their fearless ringleader).

So although a unit had already responded to the call, Gil Borsch bolted from the station, jumped into his squad car, and tore out of the parking lot (taking the turn onto the street on two wheels).

Now, perhaps it was the determination with which he hit the streets. Or perhaps it was that he knew exactly where he was going. Or maybe it was just the number of right-of-way laws he broke getting there. Whatever the contributing factors, Gil Borsch may not have been the first to respond, but he was the first to arrive on the scene.

"Officer Borsch!" Marissa cried when she saw him. "Over here!"

The lawman hustled toward the apartment, asking, "Is Billy all right?"

"No!" Dot cried. "His dad was beating him!"

"He's mad at Billy for ditching school," Casey explained.

A flash of doubt crossed Sergeant Borsch's face. He knew Mr. Pratt and his son didn't get along, but maybe the kids were exaggerating. What parent wouldn't be mad to learn their son had ditched school?

And corporal punishment was *not* against the law.

But then Casey brought the whole situation home. "He wouldn't listen to why Billy didn't go to school today." He turned to Heather. "Show him the video."

So Heather did, and after Sergeant Borsch watched the segment several times, he handed back the phone and pounded on the apartment door. "Mr. Pratt! Police! Open up!"

Two other police officers approached along the walkway, a male and a female. "Sergeant," the male said. "Didn't know you were responding. You got this?"

Sergeant Borsch glanced over, and to his relief the responding officers were *not* the partners Sammy had dubbed Squeaky and the Chick. These were useful officers. And in domestic-violence situations—whether you knew the perps or not—it was nice to have competent backup.

It also flashed through his mind that he'd gone completely rogue, breaking with procedure without even thinking about it. (And the without-even-thinking-about-it part definitely troubled him.)

Fortunately, he outranked both responding officers. "Stick around," he told them, then instructed Heather to show them the clip. And while she complied, he pounded on the apartment door again. "Open up, Leon! We're not going away!"

Moments later, the door opened and a surly Leon Pratt snarled, "This is my kid, my business."

"I want to see Billy," Sergeant Borsch told him.

"Well, goodie for you. He's not your kid." He glared at the teens on the walkway and added, "Instead of knockin' on *my* door, you should be out askin' these kids' parents what they're gonna do about their kids hangin' out at the mall instead of goin' to school! My kid told me they all ditched!"

Sergeant Borsch locked eyes with Leon Pratt. "Get Billy out here and let me see that he's okay, or what I'm going to do, Mr. Pratt, is show a video of you beating your kid to the district attorney and see if he wants to file charges against you."

Mr. Pratt's eyebrows stretched up ever so slightly. "What video?"

Heather handed her phone to Sergeant Borsch, and after the lawman had played the scene for Billy's dad, Mr. Pratt grew red in the face and shouted, "That is illegal!" He turned on Heather. "You had no right!"

Gil Borsch handed the phone back to Heather. "I'm sure the courts would have their own opinion." He again locked eyes with Billy's dad. "So it's your choice. You can go that route, or you can bring your son out here."

142

Mr. Pratt's defiant stare held for a tense fifteen seconds before it finally faltered. And as quickly as his face had turned red, it now went pale.

Reality, it appeared, had sunk in.

"Wait here," he instructed, and a full five minutes later, he finally reappeared with Billy.

"What's up?" Billy asked as he approached the doorway.

From outside the apartment, the teens stared at him. It was as though nothing had happened. He wasn't bleeding. He wasn't broken. He was just . . . Billy.

"Dude," Casey said quietly. "Let us help you."

"I'm fine," Billy said. "I shouldn't have ditched school."

Casey looked right at Billy's dad. "One of our friends is in a coma in the hospital. *That's* why we weren't at school today. Some of the *teachers* even left school. We were at the mall because we were hungry and the nurses in the ICU were sick of us taking up the waiting room."

The elder Pratt stared at Casey a minute, then frowned at Billy. "Why didn't you say so?"

Dot popped forward and cried, "He tried to!" then immediately backed down.

"And even if you didn't know," Casey told Mr. Pratt, "it's no reason to beat up your kid!" He turned to Billy. "We saw, okay? And Heather's got enough on video for proof. So stop pretending everything's okay."

"Come on, Billy," Holly coaxed. "You don't have to put up with this."

Regardless of what the other kids said to try to convince Billy, Sergeant Borsch had seen enough domestic-violence cases to know that the boy was not going to file a complaint against his father. And since the abuse had not crossed over into Billy needing medical attention, there was nothing he could legally do to intervene. So instead he switched to an unapproved (and questionably lawful) tactic:

Blackmail.

"Here's the deal, Leon," he said quietly to Mr. Pratt. "We've got some very damning evidence against you. I'm going to keep this clip on file. I'm going to document everything that happened here. And I'm going to alert the school to watch out for signs of physical trauma where your son is concerned. I can't be here twenty-four-seven, but these kids are good friends and they're not about to let this continue. So if you *don't* want to wind up in jail, if you *don't* want social services to remove your kid from your home, you will change your ways. Are we clear?"

Leon Pratt stood in the wide-open doorway, visibly feeling cornered. And knowing that a cornered man is a desperate (and often violent) man, Sergeant Borsch gave him an out. "You want to be a good dad, right? You don't want to have this kind of relationship with your kid, right? And Billy doesn't want it either. Look how he covered for you! So get some help figuring it out. The county has people who can help. It won't cost you anything but a little time."

Mr. Pratt looked down, and a long silence ensued before he heaved a sigh. And then (in a moment of unexpected candor) he said, "His mom's been tellin' me the same thing."

"Does she live here?" Sergeant Borsch asked.

Leon Pratt nodded. "She'll be home shortly."

"So talk it over with her tonight," Sergeant Borsch said. "And just to give you and your son a little space and time, what do you think about Billy spending the night with one of his friends?"

"He can stay with me," Casey offered.

Mr. Pratt nodded again, then looked at Billy. "That'd be all right."

Very quietly Billy told his dad, "Sorry I snuck out this morning. Sorry I ditched school. Sorry my phone was off. Sorry I didn't tell you about Sammy."

Mr. Pratt perked up. "*Sammy's* the one in a coma?"

Billy nodded.

Leon Pratt stared at his son a moment. "I know how much you like her." Then he let out a heavy sigh and said, "I'm sorry about . . . everything. Get your things and go be with your friends. We'll talk more tomorrow. Just *please* leave your phone on, okay?"

Billy nodded, and while he was scurrying around the apartment, stuffing overnight things (including his favorite blanket) into a pillowcase, Sergeant Borsch quietly handed Leon Pratt a social-services business card, pointing out a number he could call for family counseling.

When the door was closed again and the entourage of teens and cops was headed back toward the street, one of the backup officers walked beside Sergeant Borsch and said, "I've been out on a lot of domestic-dispute calls, sir, but I have never seen one resolved like that." He looked at the Borschman with awe. "That was incredible."

Gil Borsch frowned. "Not entirely by the book . . ."

"Maybe not," the other officer said, "but it's exactly what was needed."

Which (aside from the satisfaction of a job well done) was, for the Borschman, payday enough. He hadn't always had the respect of his colleagues. There was a time (like when he'd been dumped by his horse in the Christmas Parade) that'd he'd been the station's bona fide laughingstock. During this same time, minor infractions (like, oh, jaywalking or spitting on the sidewalk) had seemed justifiably cite-worthy.

So what had transformed him from a citation-happy, horse-bucked, blustery cop into one who could defuse a domestic dispute?

Not that there was any guarantee that Leon Pratt would follow through, but still.

How had he become a cop who commanded the awe of officers coming up the ranks?

In his heart of hearts Gil Borsch knew that it wasn't just another season on the force, and it wasn't merely the passing of time. It was learning how to listen. Finally learning how to listen. (Something both his ex-wives had begged him repeatedly to do.)

And the person who had taught him to listen?

Sammy.

Somehow, with her long, maddening asides and wild, rambling stories, she'd taught him to take a deep breath and just listen. And somehow, after years of hating teenagers, he'd learned to like, even love, a teenager.

And now here he was, surrounded by a little herd of teenagers who turned to him for help.

Maybe even *liked* him.

"Officer Borsch?" a voice was saying.

"Huh?" the lawman said.

"Did you find out who threw Sammy off the fire escape?"

It was Marissa asking, and after a quick refocus on the here and now, Sergeant Borsch shook his head. "No. Sorry. Not yet."

"Well, here," Marissa said, handing over the list they'd made. "We're hoping this will help."

The backup officers had kept walking and were now calling, "See you back at the station."

"Ten-four," Sergeant Borsch responded, then turned again to Marissa. "What is this?"

"It's a list of the people who might want to take revenge on Sammy." And after Sergeant Borsch had studied it a moment, she asked, "Can you find out which ones are in jail and which ones are out?"

He nodded, then shook the page and said, "Thank you. I was starting a list myself, but I've had . . . interruptions."

"Sorry," Billy said, clearly feeling guilty for the distraction his situation had caused.

"You, son, shouldn't feel guilty about anything." Then Sergeant Borsch frowned and said, "Actually, I was waylaid by the Nightie-Napper."

"The Nightie-Napper?" the teens cried. "What happened? Did you catch him?"

But before he could answer, Cricket and Heather asked, "What's a nightie-napper?"

Casey gave them the condensed version and then turned to Sergeant Borsch and asked, "What happened?"

So Sergeant Borsch gave his own condensed version (to cries of "Mr. *Garnucci* is the Nightie-Napper?!") and ended his story with, "So he's locked up, and once his lawyer's present, we'll also question him about last night."

"Wait," Marissa said. "You think *he* might have thrown Sammy off the stairs?"

Gil Borsch sucked on a tooth, visualizing the manager dressed as a granny. It didn't seem too likely, but Garnucci *had* attacked him with a bike. "I'll add him to your list," he said. "But not to the top of it." Then he said, "Why don't you kids go back to the hospital while I do some checking on the list."

This seemed to be the perfect line with which to make an exit, but instead of heading toward his squad car, Gil Borsch just stood there, studying Sammy's friends, sucking quietly on his tooth.

"What?" Casey finally asked after the look and the lack of movement had gotten awkward.

Gil Borsch frowned.

He knew that what he was thinking was rash.

Maybe even stupid.

These were teenagers!

And Heather had been an unbelievable thorn in his side.

Not to mention Sammy's!

But she did seem to be trying.

And she'd sure come through with that video. . . .

So, looking around at all the kids' expectant faces, Gilbert Borsch took a deep breath and decided. "Take out your phones," he said. "I'm going to give you my cell number."

After a moment of stunned silence, all at once all available phones were produced.

And after Sergeant Borsch had relayed the number, he looked around the group and said, "Do not share it with anyone. It is only for you, got it?" And after a round of *got-it*s were returned, he said, "So here's what I want you to do with it: Call me if you're in trouble, call me if you need help"—he took another deep breath—"and if you hear any news about Sammy, call me about that, too."

Then he headed to his squad car, wondering what in the world had gotten into him.

17—LANA

As the world outside was buzzing with news crews and list making, Lana sat alone in Sammy's hospital room, looking at her daughter. Like haunting calls into a canyon of regret, thoughts bounced farther and farther into the distance, carrying Lana's heart along as they drifted back in time.

"I remember when you were born," the actress whispered to her daughter. And after a long moment of silence, she said, "That seems like a lifetime ago . . . and also like yesterday."

The monitors silently tracked Sammy's vitals as she lay bandaged and unmoving but for the steady rise and fall, rise and fall of her chest.

"I wasn't always a bad mom," Lana whispered. "You may not remember, but I really, really tried." She slipped her hand over Sammy's. "Maybe I should have waited a few more years to pursue my dream. No, I *know* I should have waited. But thirty freaked me out. I went from being a teenager, to being a mother, to waitressing at Big Daddy's, to being thirty. It felt like my life was over and I'd never really had a chance to *do* anything.

"Oh, there was my short-lived move to Hollywood

after high school. I was so naïve, auditioning for parts during the day, waitressing at a diner on Sunset at night. My eyes were so full of stars!" She thought a moment as if grappling with how much to share, then said, "That's where I met your father—has he told you that? He and the band would come into the diner after doing a showcase. He was so charming and Marko was so funny. Marko had amazing hair back then, too. Full and shaggy . . . it's still strange to see him bald.

"Anyway, it's not like they didn't warn me, right? They were the Troublemakers! But I fell so hard for your dad. And then"—she heaved a sigh—"well, things fell apart, and I was left with you and a bunch of shattered dreams.

"That didn't mean I didn't love you. But I was back in Santa Martina, and it didn't take long for me to feel old and trapped and like such an embarrassing failure. Plus, I was working at a truck stop! The tips were good, but you have no idea how demeaning it was to work there! Your grandmother wanted me to take night classes so I could get on to something better, but I couldn't seem to find the time. Besides, accounting, or nursing, or secretarial skills . . . it was not where my heart was. And I was tired a lot!"

Lana paused for a moment, and then the words seemed to want to gush out. Like they'd been waiting for years to be set free. "You were not an easy child, Samantha. I know it wasn't your fault. You're like your father—curious and energetic . . . and a magnet for trouble! Nowhere was safe with you in it. Not the grocery store, not the mall, not the playground . . . You always managed to knock something over, or get a leg caught, or *tackle* someone. Why did you need to chase other kids? Why did you need to *tackle* them? Your grandmother said you were just trying to make friends, but what kind of way is that to make friends? I needed a helmet and a leash for you!" She shook her head. "You were just exhausting."

Lana was quiet for a long time. It was as if she'd arrived at a fork on a distant road and was not quite sure which way to go, and when she did at last begin again, her voice was just a whisper. "Do you remember that little one-bedroom place we rented on Hill Street after my dad left us and Mom lost the house? The three of us were crammed into what was supposedly a duplex, but it was really just half of a tiny house where the water heater was in the kitchen and the refrigerator partly blocked the doorway into the bedroom. The neighbor in the other half would be up all night playing loud music, and sometimes it'd be Darren Cole and the Troublemakers, which was really, really hard for me to take. I would be next to you in bed, trying to be quiet while I sobbed, but you would sometimes wake up anyway and ask me what was wrong and wipe my tears away with your little hands and then kiss me and tell me you loved me." She took a deep, choppy breath, then choked out, "I'm sorry about those nights. I'm sorry for making you worry. I'm sorry I let you see how depressed I was."

After another long silence, Lana began again. "Your grandmother was the one who used to sleep on the couch. Do you remember that? It's pretty funny, now that I think about it. And sometimes the two of you would sleep on that couch together. It wasn't big, but I'd come home from my shift, and there you'd be, burrowed into each other with a book dropped to the side. And when I'd try to get you to move into the bed, you'd cling to her for dear life and tell me, 'No!' "

Lana studied her daughter a moment, then said, "I think I was probably a little jealous, even back then. You and she were always such buddies. With me she was a disciplinarian. With you she was easy. And affectionate. I don't remember my mom hugging me very much when I was a kid, but you came along and suddenly she was all arms.

"And then she got into the Highrise and you were in school and getting so independent, and I . . . I was going nowhere." Lana stroked her daughter's hand. And after several minutes she said, "It was your grandmother's idea, you know. To have you stay with her in the Highrise? She was the first one to suggest it, and she did it in front of you! So of course you thought it was a big adventure." She let out a sigh. "And I thought it was only going to last a month or two. Or through the end of sixth grade at the most! I definitely thought I'd be settled and you'd be with me in Los Angeles by the time junior high started. That was my deadline. The beginning of seventh grade. You'd be starting a new school anyway, right? It made complete sense!

"But . . . it didn't work out that way." She frowned. "I know I should have called more. I know I should have come to visit more. I know I shouldn't have gotten so wrapped up in myself and what I was doing. But I did *not* abandon you to become the Gas-Away lady! I cannot believe you ever thought that, let alone said it! It was *embarrassing* to be the Gas-Away lady! I still cringe about it! But some-times you have to swallow your pride to get your foot in the door . . . especially if you have a child you're supposed to be taking care of!"

Lana sat staring at her daughter, absorbing her in a way she hadn't since Samantha had been a toddler sleeping at her side.

Who was this girl?

This . . . young lady.

How had this . . . any of this . . . happened?

"Sometimes I have trouble wrapping my mind around the fact that you're *my* daughter," she whispered. "How did you become so brave? So resourceful? When I think about the things that you've gotten yourself into . . ." The actress shuddered. "I've heard, you know. In bits and pieces over time, I've heard. And I can see *acting* those scenes, but liv-ing them? Oooo. You know how I get around rodents and blood—imagine how I'd be around corpses! Or trapped in a basement with poisonous spiders!" She fluttered a hand as if fanning away a panic attack. "I would have *died*. Or needed serious counseling! Or something! But you just went on about your life like nothing had happened. You never even mentioned it to me!"

After another long silence, Lana took a deep breath and whispered, "Please wake up, Sunshine. Please come back to me!" And then, like a main line breaking open, she threw herself forward and burst into tears.

Only there was a problem.

She couldn't really reach her daughter because the bed's guardrail was in the way.

So she frantically pulled the barricade. Pushed the barricade. Tried to find the release latch for the barricade. But (being both overwrought and not mechanically inclined) she got nowhere.

Which made her cry even harder.

And the harder she cried, the more she wanted to wrap her daughter in her arms and just hold her.

Like she had when Samantha was a little girl.

Back when she could still protect her.

And now, once again, the reality of the situation seemed too much to bear.

What if her daughter never woke up?

What if she could never tell her she was sorry?

After the flood of tears subsided and only sprinkles remained, Lana wiped her cheeks, then reached over the railing to try again to hug her daughter.

But it was awkward.

Impossible, really.

So she reached over and kissed Sammy on the forehead.

But . . . that was very unsatisfying.

And it seemed like the wrong gesture completely!

Like something you would do to an old, tired relative.

Or a corpse in a casket!

If you had the guts to kiss a corpse in a casket, that is.

Which she did not!

Unless, maybe, it was Samantha.

No!

The image gripped her heart, and she fanned away another panic attack as she whimpered, "You cannot die. Samantha, please wake up. Please!"

But her daughter didn't wake up.

And after the next flood of tears came and went, Lana stood there completely drained and overcome with fatigue. In all her double shifts at Big Daddy's, in all her long days on *Lords,* she had never, ever felt this tired.

Suddenly all she wanted was to curl up and close her eyes and go back to the time when it was just her and her daughter in the little bed on Hill Street.

Back to when she could wrap her sleeping child in her arms and feel her heartbeat steady and strong and fearless beside her.

Back to when life was mostly heartache and struggle.

But had never hurt like this.

18—THE ROTATION

After finishing his interview with Zelda Quinn and making a series of phone calls, Darren went to check on Lana and found her asleep in Sammy's bed with an arm draped over their daughter.

"Aw, Lana," Darren murmured, then marveled at how two people could even fit in the narrow bed, let alone how Lana had managed to fall asleep. (Lana was known for her requisite feather pillows and was, at the moment, crammed up against the guardrail like a board on its side, unsupported by a pillow of any kind.)

"What the . . . ?" came a voice from behind, and before Darren could turn, a nurse elbowed her way past him without so much as an excuse-me.

The nurse was wearing a Scrabble-patterned smock with various medical terms puzzled together, including such indelicate intersections as BLADDER and VOID, FLATUS and GUT, and (over the upper left front quadrant) HEART and ATTACK. "Did you turn this off?" she asked as she toggled up a switch at the side of the bed.

"No, what is it?" Darren asked.

"The movement sensor. It was turned off."

"Meaning?"

"Meaning if there had been movement, we wouldn't have been alerted." The Scrabble nurse eyed the still-sleeping Lana. "And if someone climbed in bed with the patient, we wouldn't know it."

"It's her mother," Darren explained.

"Oh, I'm aware," the nurse said, then reached across the bed and gave Lana a shake. "Ma'am. Ma'am, you're not allowed to be in the bed."

Lana's eyes fluttered open and she gave the nurse a groggy look.

"And don't jolt the patient," the Scrabble nurse instructed.

Darren, fearing that Lana might freak out at the sight of her still-unconscious daughter, hurried over to the other side of the bed and let the guardrail down. "Come on, sweetheart," he said gently. "Come on out."

"How'd you do that?" Lana asked, because even in the fog of an interrupted sleep cycle, it registered that Darren had retracted the railing with no effort at all.

"Come on," Darren coaxed. "Easy . . ."

"I'm serious, Darren," Lana said as she slid out. "How did you do that?"

So he dutifully put the rail back up, then demonstrated how to release it.

"No more getting in with her," the nurse instructed. "There's a sensor that'll alarm."

"I set off an alarm?" Lana asked, looking back and forth between the nurse and Darren.

"No," Nurse Scrabble said as she inspected the IV bag, "but next time you will."

Having slept through the initial part of the whole sensor discussion, Lana didn't really understand the distinction. She was also distracted by the back of the nurse's shirt (which had DUODENUM intersecting with CONSTIPATION, GALLBLADDER, and BILE) and was simply glad to see the tasteless shirt exit the room. "This is a strange place," she whispered after the Scrabble nurse was gone.

Darren (being both male and a rock guy) could see the humor in the shirt, but not in the situation. Instead of dwelling on it, though, he focused on the positive. "I've got some good news," he said, putting an arm around Lana's waist. "A pediatric neurosurgeon at Johns Hopkins is going to confer with Dr. Jha about Sammy's case. His name is Dr. Kumar, and he is one of the top coma specialists in the world."

"Really?" Lana asked, suddenly awake. "When?"

Darren checked the battery level of his cell phone. "Sometime this evening. He said he'll arrange to have the brain scans sent so he can review them before he speaks with Dr. Jha."

"*You* talked to him? How?"

Darren nodded. "Friend of a friend of a friend." He slipped his phone away and said, "Although why a neurosurgeon would be a fan of mine is something I don't quite understand."

Lana gave him a sweet smile. "Well, I do. And thank you."

"It doesn't change anything," he said gently.

"But I feel better knowing that someone with some credibility is involved." She looked past the curtain, then dropped her voice. "This place doesn't give me much confidence."

Which, for Darren, was it in a nutshell. And while not wanting to alarm Lana by adding fuel to the fire, he did have his concerns and was not about to leave Sammy without supervision.

Even though ostensibly there was nothing to supervise.

And theoretically there was nothing he could do.

It didn't matter.

"If you want to take a break, I'll sit here for a while," he told Lana.

But Lana pulled two chairs together and sat down defiantly. "I'm going nowhere," she said.

Now, with Lana wanting for the past fourteen years to be going anywhere *but* nowhere, the irony of her statement hung for a moment in the air.

But only for a moment.

Then Darren sat down beside her and held her hand, grateful she was there.

Grateful to be with her, going nowhere.

Out in the waiting room, a rotation of sorts had occurred. Having captured the footage of a lifetime, Zelda Quinn and her cameraman had beat a hasty exit to get at least a short segment ready in time for the five o'clock broadcast, and the full piece together for the six o'clock. The teachers (and former vice principal) had also left, assuring one another they'd be in touch should they hear any news.

And finally the oddball adults had left the waiting room (but not until they'd each inscribed a message on the silky-smooth fabric of the lone unicorn). Justice Jack had jumped onto his High Roller in pursuit of "Commissioner Borsch" to see where his talents as a superhero could best be put to use, and Madame Nashira and Slammin' Dave had both piled back into André's car, deciding that waiting could be done just as well in their respective places of employment.

But as the trio rolled across town, André (who had also missed lunch and was suddenly famished) had an unexpected hankering. "Anyone else feel like Italian food?" he asked.

The question surprised even him because André was not a socializer. Especially not with tenants. He'd learned many years ago that getting chummy with residents was asking for trouble. Before you knew it, they'd want favors. Or deadline extensions. Or free rent.

But aside from the potential follies of fraternizing with Gina, he'd also tossed the question out there for Dave's consideration.

What had possessed him?

He didn't fraternize with men in bright blue boots!

He just didn't.

So the minute the Italian-food suggestion made it past his cigar stub, André wished he could take it back.

He needn't have worried, though, because both his

neighbor and his tenant declined. And the idea might have been dropped entirely, but after letting Gina out at her House of Astrology on Main Street (where the astrologer hoped to divine some information regarding Sammy's future) and then pulling into his usual parking space near the Heavenly, Slammin' Dave asked, "Have you tried Mindy's?"

"Mindy's?" André replied, the car in park, but still idling.

Dave got out of the car and pointed. "It's around the corner on Main. Where Alphy's used to be? Best Italian food I've ever had."

"Thanks, man," André said, and while Dave (and his bright blue boots) walked away, André sat in his car with his engine (and his mind) running. Why had he even asked about Italian food? He had no time to go out!

He had a hotel to run.

He had . . . well, things to do.

Or, at least, read.

Besides, it was between mealtimes. The place might not even be open.

But something about the events of the day, something about the reminder that life was finite (and always much too short, even if you were lucky enough to get old) kept him sitting in the car with the engine idling.

Plus, he realized with a helpless sort of sadness, he just didn't want to be alone.

So he put the car back in gear and puttered away from the Heavenly and around the corner to Mindy's Cucina d'Italia, where he parked curbside.

André found that the restaurant *was* open, but it was empty. And feeling alone to begin with, he almost turned around. Eating alone in an empty restaurant was sure not going to make him feel any less alone!

But the little bell on the door had jingled, and now a woman appeared from the kitchen area. "Don't be shy," she said with dancing eyes. "The food is good!" And before he could find a way to resist, she'd secured him at a corner table with a menu. "Something to drink?" she asked. "Water? Or maybe a glass of Chianti?"

Coffee would have been more his style. Or maybe a beer. But wine? After working at the Heavenly for so many years, wine had a very negative association (caused by the recycled state in which it was left in hallways or corners for him to clean up).

But the setting here, with its checkered tablecloths and lacy half curtains, was nothing like the Heavenly. And the truth was, nothing went with Italian food like a good red wine.

"How about a glass of Chianti on the house," the woman said with a warm smile. "Seems like you could use one."

She returned moments later with the wine and a basket of bread. And after leaving him alone for a few minutes to consider the menu choices, she appeared again and looked at him expectantly.

Perhaps it was the wine (which was already half gone), but instead of just placing his order, André asked, "How's the lasagna?" and (to his bewilderment and extreme embarrassment) his eyes began stinging with tears.

"It's my grandmother's recipe," the woman assured him. "It's beyond wonderful."

He handed back the menu. "Then that's what I'll have."

She took the menu but paused to study him. "I know it's none of my business, but . . . are you okay?"

He nodded.

"Are you new in town?"

He shook his head, and since he couldn't seem to get any words past the lump in his throat, the woman backed away and disappeared into the kitchen.

André, of course, felt like a complete fool, but when the woman returned with the steaming plate of lasagna, she seemed to have nothing but sympathy. She placed his meal in front of him, then slid into the chair across from him and said, "Do you want to tell me about her?"

"Her?" André asked.

"Well, it must be a girl, right?"

André looked away, and even though the situation was not what the woman was thinking, his head bobbed.

"So tell me about her. This girl who's made you so sad."

And since they were alone and the wine was now gone, he studied her kind brown eyes, then took a bite of the best lasagna he'd ever tasted and began. "Her name is Sammy."

19—OHIO?

As the teens began the walk from Billy's house back toward the hospital, Marissa was gripped with a horrible, heart-stopping thought: If her mother followed through with her plan to move them to Ohio this summer, it would create a void. A void that Heather would fill.

Heather had always been resourceful and determined, and now that Sammy had "celebrity connections," Heather would do whatever it took to become Sammy's new best friend. She'd already shown obvious signs of it, and with Marissa out of the way, it would be easy! Sure, Holly would put up roadblocks for a while, but she had other things going on. Like dogs and becoming a vet and denying her undeniable crush on Preston Davis.

And Dot wouldn't know how to stop her—she was way too nice.

And Casey? He used to stand up to Heather, but since that trip to Las Vegas he was always telling everyone to go easy on her.

No, without someone truly committed, the resistance would fall pretty quickly.

She was the only person who would stand firm and stop

Heather, or in no time Heather would become Sammy's new best friend.

And so, like a switch suddenly flipped, Marissa knew what she had to do. "Gotta go!" she announced to the rest of the teens, then took off running.

"Wait! Where are you going?" Holly hollered after her.

"Gotta get Mikey!" she shouted (or, rather, lied) at full volume.

"Who?" Heather called after her.

Marissa spun and yelled, "You know, BLUBBER BOY?" then doubled her speed and didn't look back.

Now it *was* true that since Yolanda McKenze had moved Marissa and Mikey out of their mansion on East Jasmine and into a modest condo in town, Marissa had been on the hook to walk her brother home from after-school care, because it ended before Yolanda got off work at six. Today, however, Yolanda had told Marissa that she would rearrange things with her new employer so Marissa could be with Sammy.

Even though it meant losing valuable time at work.

Even though (as Yolanda had made very clear) they really, really, *really* needed the money.

"Mom!" Marissa shouted as she barged through the condo door.

"What?" Yolanda appeared in the small front room with a wooden spoon in hand. "What happened?"

"We cannot move to Ohio!"

"What's this about?" Yolanda asked, returning quickly to the kitchen.

Marissa dumped her backpack and followed. She was

momentarily distracted by the mouth-watering aroma of sautéed onions, but she forced herself to stay on topic. "Heather! She's already taking over!"

Yolanda added a can of stewed tomatoes to the saucepan. "What are you talking about?"

"Sammy!"

"But . . . is Sammy awake?" She nodded at a small television on the counter, which was tuned into KSMY's five o'clock report. "The news made it sound like she was still unconscious."

"She is! But Heather's totally positioning herself to take over!"

"Take over *what*?"

"My spot as Sammy's best friend!"

"How can you be worried about that when your friend is in a coma?"

Marissa muted the TV (which was broadcasting news that had nothing to do with Sammy) and gave her mother an exasperated look. "I'm talking about after she wakes up! Heather's already moving in. She's taking video and saving the day! She's calling the shots and snowing Officer Borsch! She's fooling everyone into believing she's changed!"

Yolanda had the urge to tell her daughter that a coma was a much bigger thing to worry about than Heather's manipulations. And that there was no guarantee Sammy would wake up at all.

Instead, what popped out of her mouth was, "Toss the salad, would you? And set the table? And tell me what video you're talking about and how Heather is snowing Officer Borsch."

So Marissa got busy tossing and started talking. And when she was done relaying the drama, she said, "So we can't move. We just can't."

"Sweetheart," her mother said with a sympathetic sigh, "has it occurred to you that *Sammy* might move?"

"No! She's happy at Hudson's! Why would she move?"

"Because her *parents* will want her to. Because from what you've told me, Lana and Darren are headed for the altar, and once that happens, they'll want to be together as a family." She shook her head. "Because there's no way they'll leave Sammy alone after this, and I sure can't see either of them moving to Santa Martina."

Marissa didn't like that thought.

Didn't like it one bit.

"Sammy belongs *here*," she said at last. "Not in Los Angeles! Or Las Vegas! Can you imagine her having to live in Las Vegas?"

Mrs. McKenze simply gave a little shrug as she put pasta into a pot of boiling water.

Marissa realized that they'd gotten way off track, and, thinking reinforcements would help, she asked, "Where's Mikey?"

"Right here," the nine-year-old said, then stepped out from around the corner.

"You don't have to spy," Mrs. McKenze scolded.

"But he's Spy Guy," Marissa said, giving her brother a knowing grin. "Hey! That reminds me . . . Justice Jack is back!"

"He's back?" Mikey squealed. "For good?"

"I don't know about for good," Marissa said, placing

utensils around the plates she'd already put on their small kitchen table. "He's here for Sammy. To help figure out who put her in a coma."

Mrs. McKenze sighed, then muttered, "How can anyone want to stay in a town where a fool like that roams the streets?"

"He's not a fool!" Mikey cried. "Justice Jack is *awesome*." He stepped farther into the kitchen. "How can you want to *leave*?"

"We really have to talk about it, Mom," Marissa said quietly. "I don't want to move, Mikey doesn't want to move—"

Yolanda McKenze's eyebrows knit together. "Because of Justice Jack?"

"No! Because he's finally got some friends!" Marissa said. "Because Hudson's been great for him, and where are you going to find another Hudson? Because he doesn't want to live with me if I'm miserable, and I'm going to be completely miserable if you move us to Ohio!" She suddenly turned to Mikey. "There are no fish in Ohio."

"No fish?" Mikey gasped (as fancy fish in an aquarium were still his favorite thing in the whole wide world).

"There are too fish in Ohio!" Mrs. McKenze cried. She turned to her daughter. "What sort of tactic is that?"

Marissa plopped into a chair and flicked her eyebrows up. "Dirty."

"So tell him the truth!"

Marissa sighed. "Okay. There *are* fish." Then she quickly added, "They serve them filleted. With soggy rice pilaf. And Brussels sprouts."

"Marissa!"

"Fine," the teen grumbled as she slumped in her chair. "There are fish. In tanks. Swimming." She eyed her brother. "But they're nowhere near as pretty as the ones you can get out here."

"Marissa!"

"Look," Marissa sighed. "We don't want to move." She gave her brother a recruiting look. "Am I right, Mikey?"

Mikey's face furrowed. "I thought we *had* to move."

"We do!" Mrs. McKenze said. "We would have moved already, but there's a lot of . . . of legal work that needs to be wrapped up. And I wanted you to be able to finish out the school year!" She gave her son a pleading look. "Don't you want to get to know your grandparents better? Aren't you excited about meeting new people and getting a fresh start?"

Marissa (still slumping) crossed her arms. "No, we're not."

Mikey's arms crossed, too. "Do we *have* to?"

Yolanda McKenze sighed as she looked from one child to the other. She knew the Ohio Plan was a desperate one, but *everything* she'd done since she'd bailed her husband out of a Las Vegas jail had been some desperate form of triage. Some way to stop the bleeding. In their finances, in their reputation, and in her marriage.

Still, as desperately as she'd tried to save each, none had survived. And as much as returning to Ohio would in some ways be the ultimate failure, it was a safe (and cheap) place to regroup. And staying in this town with the gossips and the gambler and the grotesquely successful in-laws was too much for her.

Way. Too. Much.

But in truth, she *couldn't* just up and move to Ohio with the children until a custody agreement was worked out, or a judge granted her permission. Permission her soon-to-be ex was fighting tooth and nail.

Still, weary as she was from all the stress, embarrassment, and arguments (not to mention the humiliation of clerking for little more than minimum wage), Yolanda McKenze refused to let on to the children how bad things really were. She used words like *regroup* and *downsize* and *adjust*, and avoided calling their father the names he deserved.

Oh, the names he deserved!

"Mom, where are you right now?"

Yolanda was shaken from her thoughts by her daughter's voice. "In a land far, far away," she said with a sigh, then crumpled into a chair beside Marissa. "My parents moved us when I was a sophomore. It was only one town over, but I had to go to a different high school. I hated it."

Marissa's eyebrows shot up. "So? You know exactly what I mean!"

"But, honey, sometimes it's good to start over. And you'll be *starting* high school, not ripped out of the middle of it."

"Mom, it's the same thing! And what about Mikey? He's in the *middle* of elementary school!"

"So we really *don't* have to move?" Mikey asked again, moving closer.

Yolanda took a deep breath and held her son's gaze. In the past few months he had become a happy boy. There was no doubt that Hudson's influence and support throughout their family crisis had been wonderful, but it was more than that. For the first time ever, her son had a real friend. Little, adorable, bright-eyed Lucero. Instead of moping, Michael had become a chatterbox about Lucero this and Lucero that.

Perhaps if he'd been a different sort of child, she would have been more confident that he would move on to new friends in their new location. But Michael was . . . Michael. And he'd had a really rough few years.

She looked away and said, "I thought you liked Ohio."

"Not to *move* to!" Mikey cried. "I want to stay here!"

Marissa sat up and said, "I was Mikey's age when Sammy and I became best friends, Mom. It's a really formative time."

"Formative?" Yolanda asked, raising an eyebrow Marissa's way. "And when did you start psychoanalyzing things?" But the comment did resonate with her—perhaps because she regretted how pushing aside warning signs in favor of work had likely created so many issues with Michael. Or perhaps it was because she was remembering her own best friend from third grade. A girl named Susan, whose family had moved away at the end of sixth grade.

Plus, wasn't divorce hard enough on the kids without also ripping apart their friendships?

"Mom?" Marissa asked, because Yolanda's mind was clearly wandering off again. "What are you thinking?"

Yolanda sighed, then pulled Mikey in and said, "I'm thinking that it's a parent's job to make the right decisions for their kids, even if those decisions are hard and not popular. I'm thinking that I really don't want to live in this little condo in this little town full of gossips. And I'm thinking that a fresh start would be good for *me* . . . but that maybe I need to think about all of this some more." She shook her head. "If we stay in Santa Martina, we won't be moving back to East Jasmine or anywhere like it. You understand that, right? This is probably as good as it's going to get for a while."

"I don't care!" Marissa cried, and Mikey said, "I *like* it here! Way better than the big house."

Yolanda studied him. "You do?"

"Way!" he cried. "There's no big hill. I can ride my bike! It's close to the park and the mall and school and Hudson's . . . it's *way* better here!"

Yolanda was suddenly struck by the futility of her previous financial pursuits. How all the adult trappings they'd chased for years had nothing whatsoever to do with the happiness of her children.

And really, it *was* about time the children came first.

"You're really thinking about it?" Marissa asked.

Yolanda gave her a little smile and then a little nod. "No promises, but yes, I will think about it."

"Oh, Mom!" Marissa squealed as she wrapped her in a hug. "You're the best!"

Mikey also squeezed her tight, and as she hugged them back, Yolanda felt the weight and worry of the past months lift.

Somehow they would get through this. As humiliating and dire as things were right now, they would get better.

And as she held her kids tight, there was one clear and present thought that made every other worry seem small.

At least her daughter wasn't in a coma.

20—THE PLEA

Wanting desperately to tell Sammy about the Maybe-Not-Moving-to-Ohio Conversation because (unconscious or not) this was something her best friend would definitely want to hear, Marissa was tempted to make excuses and bolt from the condo. But the spaghetti dinner her mom had cooked smelled so good, and (for someone who had, until recently, survived on frozen meals while her parents worked endless hours) this whole "family dinner" thing her mom had started was . . . nice.

Even if it wasn't the whole family.

Even if it meant doing dishes afterward (instead of simply throwing the microwave trays away).

She and Mikey had settled on a cleanup system where Marissa washed (because Mikey was awful at it and took forever) and Mikey dried (something he did with inexplicable speed and efficiency).

It had also become a time when they talked.

Well, mostly Mikey talked, but sometimes Marissa did, too, and she'd discovered not only that her brother was hilarious, but that he had become her steadfast champion. That he was willing to do battle with whoever gave her a hard time. And somewhere in the sudsing sessions she'd also realized that, although Mikey would always be younger than she was, he wouldn't always be smaller; one day he'd be taller and stronger, and anyone who messed with her would have him to answer to.

So Marissa loved the homemade meals and didn't mind the dishes, but tonight she was mostly glad she'd stuck around because she didn't miss the six o'clock news. "Look!" Mikey cried as they were clearing the table. "It's Justice Jack!"

The TV was still on in the kitchen and Marissa un-muted it as quickly as she could, but although the screen showed an image of the self-proclaimed superhero, it was Zelda Quinn's voice that came through the speakers, not Jack Wesley's. ". . . is back in Santa Martina to help get to the bottom of this horrible crime, and, as you can see, he's not alone in his support." As the shot panned around the ICU waiting room, Zelda's voice continued. "The girl who was hurled three stories and is clinging to life in Community Hospital's intensive-care unit is no ordinary teen. According to these fans, both young and adult, she's something of a superhero herself. One who has quietly and consistently helped her community without fanfare or even public recognition. Instead of wearing the flashy get-up of a traditional superhero, she disguises herself as an ordinary teen and keeps a low profile."

"That's you!" Mikey squealed, pointing at Marissa's bowed head in the panning footage.

"Look at all those bears," Yolanda whispered.

"What are you guys doing?" Mikey asked.

"Shhhh!" Marissa hissed.

So the kitchen fell quiet again, except for Zelda's voice. "Her friends and even the ICU staff are writing messages to this special girl as an extension or *adaptation* of something her boyfriend started with her shoes."

"They're showing her *shoes*?" Marissa gasped as Sammy's high-tops displayed on the screen. "Oh, that is creepy."

"So who is this girl?" Zelda asked. "This surreptitious superhero in the scribed shoes? It seems only fitting that her name is also a deception—a nickname that would have you believing she is something she's not. It also seems fitting that her father—who wears similar shoes—was, until recently, a well-kept secret himself."

"Sammy's going to hate this," Marissa whispered, because Zelda Quinn was clearly winding up for the pitch.

"Was he there?" Yolanda asked, and Mikey added, "Darren Cole?" like he was totally on top of everything that was going on.

Marissa nodded, and again she said, "Sammy's going to hate this."

"I'd do it if I were him," Yolanda hurried to whisper. "I'd do anything to catch who did it."

Marissa glanced over, and sure enough, the emotion she'd heard in her mother's voice was backed up by glassy eyes.

Then Zelda threw her curveball, starting with a shot of Darren's shoes. "Maybe you know him as the man who sang 'Dusk Before Dawn' or 'Watertower' or any of the hits that have been a soundtrack in so many of our lives"—the camera panned up to a full shot of Darren's face as the voice-over continued—"but today Darren Cole says he's not a rock star or a Troublemaker. He's just a dad. A man who needs your help."

And then Darren's voice was in. "I can't even begin to explain how special Sammy is," he said. "But if you're a parent, just imagine it's your kid that's hurt. Please help. Think back to last night. Talk to your friends. If you know anything, saw anything, have heard anything, speak up. I'm begging you, please speak up."

"That's it?" Marissa whispered when the shot cut away.

"That's enough," Yolanda sniffed.

Contact numbers appeared on-screen as Zelda Quinn made a final in-studio plea to help "break the case wide open," and then a commercial for Mattress Mania's big-big-big weekend sale began blaring.

Marissa zapped off the TV. "I've got to get back to the hospital," she said softly.

"I'm going with you," Mikey said.

Yolanda nodded. "So am I."

Then Mikey added, "And not 'cause of Justice Jack, either."

Marissa studied her brother. "No?"

He gave a little shrug. "Sammy's my friend, too. And all the stuff she's done?" He shook his head. "She never even wore a cape."

Mikey McKenze wasn't the only one who did a double take at the sight of Justice Jack on TV. "Hey, Sarge!" a young officer called from the police station's break room. "You're gonna want to see this!"

Gil Borsch hurried to join the cluster of officers gathered around the television, and immediately cringed at the sight of the flamboyant (and unauthorized) crime fighter. "You gotta be kidding me!" he groaned. "Like I haven't got enough to deal with?"

And when the plea from Darren ran, the Borschman (already choked up from seeing Sammy's shoes) quickly exited the break room with a gruff "Great, just great. Now the phone'll be ringin' off the hook with leads to nowhere," and returned to his desk to continue with his dissection of Marissa's list.

To his disgust he'd already learned that most of the perps Sammy had been instrumental in catching were (incredibly) flying free. Or, at least, out on parole. And the ones who weren't . . . Well, gangsters had a reputation for ordering hits from behind bars.

As did mobsters.

So the task of analyzing and researching the List had been alternately sobering and horrifying. Especially with the breadth and magnitude of the crimes Sammy had managed to solve consolidated onto one sheet. While individually her involvement in each case had been impressive (albeit terrifying for the dangers she'd faced), collectively it was mind-boggling.

How had she managed to get tangled up in all of these cases?

How had she figured them out?

How had she *survived*?

And with the chilling thought that perhaps she would not survive after all, Gil Borsch redoubled his efforts, certain that the teens were right.

Somewhere on the List was the key to who had done this to Sammy.

Aside from those attending the box-wine party on the fifth floor of the Highrise (where the wrinkled residents were completely oblivious to the removal of their besieged manager), and aside from the mob of teens (which had grown in size and relocated to Cheezers Pizza, where overhead televisions conveyed what they'd missed at the hospital), there was a young girl on Cypress Street and an old woman in Sisquane who also saw the broadcast.

The young girl (recognizing Sammy's shoes) informed her mother that she wanted to go see Sammy immediately, and that she wanted to bring her sheepdog.

The old woman (recognizing Sammy's friends and the *style* of the shoes) didn't need parental permission. She simply set off to the hospital on foot, with her two-hundred-pound pet pig, Penny, walking along beside her.

Now, Mr. Jan DeVries had been in regular contact with his daughter Dot (or, really, Margaret, as he used her real name, not her nickname). And having learned from his daughter that she would not be coming home for dinner, he decided to deliver some goodies to the group of teens to sustain them during their vigil.

He also hoped to obtain some more definitive information regarding Sammy's condition from adults who were sure to be hanging around, but that was secondary to wanting to support his daughter and her friends.

Friends who'd shown themselves to be true-blue.

If not a little wild.

But that was okay.

Fourteen wasn't so long ago that he couldn't remember what it was like, or how good friends at that age made all the difference in the world.

So down the road he went in his bright green DeVries Nursery delivery truck with a bag of Dutch treats in a sack at his side. And as he tooled down the road that led from Sisquane to Santa Martina, he spied something up ahead.

Something that did not belong in his lane.

"No," he said, leaning forward for a better look. "Not again!"

But a better look was really not necessary. Quite simply, there was only one hunched-over old lady who would walk a monstrous pig down the highway.

"Lucinda," Jan DeVries called after he'd pulled over ahead of her and was heading toward her.

The old woman stopped short and held on to her black velvet hat as she straightened enough to look at him. "You again?" she asked, then continued on her way. "Still haven't found your manners, I see."

"I'm sorry . . . *Mrs. Huntley,*" the Dutchman said as she moseyed past him. And then, certain that her age or the heat or simply her visual focus had disoriented her, he told her, "You've taken a wrong turn, *ja?*"

"They've moved the road to Santa Martina?" she asked. "Since when?"

"You can't possibly be walking to Santa Martina!" Jan DeVries exclaimed.

"Oh, can't I?" the old woman said, turning a blue eye up to challenge him. Then she spoke to her pig (who'd been distracted by the earthy aroma of the Dutchman's jeans). "Come along, Penny."

Now, Jan DeVries was familiar with stubborn.

After all, he came from hardy Dutch stock.

But this was something else entirely. Something even he, with all his vast experience in stubborn, didn't know how to handle.

"Mrs. Huntley!" he called (as she'd continued her trek and was already past the truck).

When she didn't respond, he shook his head and muttered, "Why in the world . . . ," but then it clicked. The last time he'd been in this situation, Sammy had been inside the truck.

As the recollection flooded back to him, he remembered how much Sammy had done for the old woman.

How she had saved Mrs. Huntley's property.

And her pig.

And if there's one thing Jan DeVries knew for sure, it was that, good or bad, the stubborn never forget.

"You're going to the hospital, *ja*?" he asked when he caught up to her.

She eyed him again. "If that's where you're headed, you could offer a lady a lift, you know."

"But . . . they won't let a pig inside the hospital!"

"Oh, won't they now?"

"No! They won't!"

"Penny has special powers, you know. Healing powers."

Jan DeVries weighed his options and concluded that he couldn't in good conscience just leave Lucinda Huntley to walk into town. It was miles and miles away. Even *he* wouldn't walk it.

(He would bike it, sure, but what self-respecting Dutchman wouldn't?)

So his choice was clear, and at last he caved.

"Let me give you a lift," he sighed.

"Why, *thank you*, young man," she said (with questionable sincerity). "I'll ride in back with Penny." She gave him a coy little smile as she adjusted her hat. "Like I did before."

And rather than worry about transport laws or potential consequences, Jan DeVries simply lowered the truck's lift gate and powered the woman and her pig up, up, up, and inside.

Then he closed them in tight, climbed into the cab, and headed for town.

In addition to Sammy's friends, there was one other significant person who had seen the six o'clock news.

He had changed his hair and glasses, was wearing newly swiped blue scrubs, and was just biding his time in the hospital cafeteria when the famous rock star made his plea.

As soon as it was over, he stood and quickly bussed his tray.

He needed to end this.

End this now.

21—DUSTY MIKE

While Jan DeVries was dealing with Lucinda Huntley and her pet pig, Janet Keltner was *also* trying to convince someone not to bring her pet to the hospital. "Elyssa. Honey," she said to her young daughter, "they won't let you bring a sheepdog inside."

But like Lucinda Huntley, Elyssa Keltner was not so easily dissuaded. "But Sammy loves Winnie! And Winnie wakes me up every morning with kisses! I'm sure she can wake Sammy up, too!"

Janet Keltner cringed at the thought of Winnie's monstrous tongue lapping at poor Sammy's face. "They won't let Winnie in, sweetheart. Winnie stays home."

"Mo-om," Elyssa said (with a distinct whinny), but then a *rat-a-tat-tat . . . tat-tat* at the door completely redirected the young girl's focus. "It's Dusty Mike!" she cried, and raced to open the door.

"Dusty Mike" Poe stood on the Keltners' porch with a heavy heart and an ancient hoe. "Evenin', Lyssie," he rasped, and then over the young girl's head he asked Janet Keltner, "Have you heard?"

A gravedigger by trade, Dusty Mike worked as a

groundskeeper at the cemetery. His vocal cords had been permanently damaged while he was trapped (and left to die) inside a crypt. And with his voice, his odd manner, his uneven gait, and his raven-like appearance, Mike Poe often unintentionally frightened people.

But Janet Keltner knew him to be a kind, gentle soul. She called him the graveyard's guardian angel, as he was someone who watched over (and cared very much for) the dead.

She also knew exactly why he was now asking what he was asking.

"We're on our way over to the hospital now," she told him. "Do you want to come with us?"

Dusty Mike nodded.

So Janet put the dog out, locked the house, and hurried toward the driveway. "The hoe stays here, Mike," she instructed, after which he grudgingly hid the ancient tool behind shrubbery for safekeeping.

At the hospital, the threesome found the ICU waiting room to be strangely quiet. "I can't believe nobody's here," Janet whispered. "On the news it looked like the place was packed!"

Nurse Scrabble (who was on her way out for a quick smoke) happened to overhear the comment. "It's the first time all day," she said, then stopped short. "Are you here to see Sammy Keyes?"

Janet Keltner smiled. "Yes, we are."

"No one under twelve permitted," the nurse said, eyeing Elyssa. Then she raised an eyebrow at Janet. "And don't try to tell me she's twelve." And before Janet could utter a word, Nurse Scrabble called, "Age alert!" toward the nurses' station and went on her way.

"Darn," Janet Keltner whispered. "I knew that, too. I'm just not thinking straight!"

"I'll watch Lyssie if you want to go," Dusty Mike offered.

Janet thought a moment, then asked her daughter, "Is there something you want me to tell Sammy?"

"Tell her to wake up!" Elyssa said.

"Okay," her mother laughed. "I will." And after stopping by the nurses' station (where she learned Sammy was "stable" and that "the family" was consulting with doctors), she headed down to Room 411, where Marko was sitting, alone.

"Hi," Janet said, and after the two had introduced themselves and exchanged their connection to Sammy, Marko said, "Hey, I need to go find some coffee. It's been a long day. If Darren and Lana show up while I'm gone, could you tell them I'll be right back?"

"Sure," Janet said, and then was suddenly alone in the room.

Now, Janet Keltner worked in a nursing home, so seeing people dying (or dead) was nothing new to her. And although a person who is exposed to it day in and day out develops a certain tolerance to the end-of-life experience, all her years at the nursing home did nothing to prepare her for the slug of emotions that hit when she turned her focus on Sammy.

She had no idea Sammy would be so covered in gauze. Or seem so helpless.

So . . . small.

Maybe it was all the teddy bears arranged around her, but suddenly Sammy didn't seem that much older than her own daughter.

"Elyssa is right outside," she whispered, trying to sound upbeat. "They won't let her in because she's too young, but she's here and she says to tell you to wake up. Actually," she said, fighting through the growing lump in her throat, "she wanted to bring Winnie to *lick* you awake. Funny, huh?"

But to Janet it wasn't funny at all.

This was . . . tragic.

And although she wanted to say more, the lump was now extreme and there were tears forming, so she simply kissed Sammy on the forehead and escaped the room, grateful that the rules had prevented Elyssa from coming inside.

On the way back to the ICU waiting room, Janet Keltner took a few minutes to compose herself, then sat with her daughter while Dusty Mike checked in at the nurses' station and took his turn.

And the gravedigger might have had the same reaction to Sammy's state as Janet had, but what helped him transition from the Sammy he knew to the one dwarfed by gauze and tubes and teddy bears was the distraction of another person in the room. A man in blue scrubs, rearranging Sammy's pillow.

"How is she?" Mike asked.

Dusty Mike was not surprised by the man's reaction to the sound (or sight) of him. As hard as he tried not to invoke it, fear (followed by a polite attempt at covering up that fear) seemed to be people's unavoidable reaction to him.

Which was the main reason he kept to himself.

And seemed to have most of his conversations with the dead.

"She's the same," the man replied, then quickly excused himself and left the room.

So, although still sobering, the sight of his young friend wasn't as jolting as it might have been. Having someone be shocked at the sight of *him* helped him, somehow, to be not so shocked at the sight of Sammy.

"Hello, friend," the gravedigger said after he'd stood by silently for a minute. "Las' time we saw each other in the hospital, *I* was the one in the bed an' you was the one visitin'." And after another moment of reflection, he leaned a little closer and said, "I know you can hear me. I know 'cause I've been where you are. Somewhere between earth and angels. It's not a bad place, is it? I was ready to let go of earth, but it was your voice that made me hold on. Did I ever tell you that? I could hear you when we was down there in the crypt. I was all but gone, but I could hear you, and it made me want to come back." He took a choppy breath, then whispered, "So if you're considerin' lettin' go, don't. There's lots of people here who want you back. Includin' me."

Now, for anyone who knew Dusty Mike and knew the history of Sammy's courageous determination to find and save him, this would have been a touching scene.

To Lana Keyes, however, finding a strange, raven-like man leaning over her daughter was terrifying.

"What are you doing?" she cried. "Get away from my daughter!"

"Sorry, ma'am," he said, hobbling away quickly.

But having gotten an even better look at the grave-digger, Lana Keyes was now certain that the man was in her daughter's room for nefarious purposes. "Help!" she screamed as he hobbled from the room. "Somebody, help!"

With enough volume and drama to raise the dead (although, again regrettably, not her own daughter), Lana's cries were answered immediately.

Nurse Faith (who had happily accepted a double shift) was the first to skid in. "What's wrong?!"

"Stop him!" Lana cried, pointing a shaky finger in the direction of Dusty Mike, who was retreating down the hallway.

"Stop him!" Nurse Faith cried at a colleague covered in rainbows, then grabbed a nearby laundry cart to help corral the man.

And then (just back from her break) Nurse Scrabble joined in the action.

Dusty Mike was surrounded.

Lana, who had hurried back to Sammy's bedside, wasted no time using her phone to call 911. And after frantically describing the situation (as only an overwrought drama queen could), she disconnected, certain she'd saved her daughter's life.

Then Nurse Scrabble entered the room. "Why, exactly, are we stopping that man?" she asked.

"He was hovering over my daughter! I think he's the one who attacked her and was here to finish the job!"

"Ummm . . . according to a woman in the waiting room, he's a friend of your daughter's?"

"A *friend*? That man is a *friend*?"

Nurse Scrabble shrugged. "According to the woman in the waiting room. Her little girl says so, too." She came farther into the room. "Is there any sign of . . . anything?" She rounded the curtain and studied the monitors, then checked Sammy over. "Was there any *specific* reason you—" And then she noticed something.

The movement sensor was, once again, turned off.

"Did you do this?" Nurse Scrabble asked, pointing to the switch.

"Did I do what?"

"Turn off the motion sensor."

"Why would I do that?"

Nurse Scrabble eyed her skeptically. "So you could crawl back in bed with her?"

"No!" And then (realizing the implication) Lana gasped. "Are you calling me a liar?"

"So maybe there's a short circuit in the system," Nurse Scrabble said (totally avoiding the question).

"Or maybe that man turned it off!"

The women stared at each other until Nurse Scrabble finally said, "Okay, well, look. Your daughter is fine."

"How can you *say* that? She's in a coma!"

Nurse Scrabble took a deep breath. "She's as fine as she was before her friend came to visit."

"And turned off the sensor so he could kill her!"

"Ma'am, please. I understand that you are upset, but there's no sense in making accusations. Do you want to talk to him? Straighten this whole thing out?"

But rather than do as the nurse suggested, Lana said, "Why aren't there restrictions on who can come in here? Why isn't it family only? Why isn't someone overseeing the activity here?" Then she added, "And *why* are you allowed to wear a shirt that has HEART intersecting with ATTACK? It's insensitive and completely tasteless!" She sniffed the air. "And *why* does it smell like cigarettes in here?"

Nurse Scrabble raised an eyebrow and tried her own avoidance tactic. "How did your consult with Dr. Jha and that specialist go?"

Lana looked away. After she and Darren had viewed images of Sammy's brain on a computer (where eye sockets were visible and, in a word, creepy), and after listening to both doctors' opinions, the conclusion from the consultation had been a maddening wait-and-see.

That's the best either had to offer.

Wait and see.

"Look, Mrs. Cole," the nurse said sympathetically, "I know this is hard. We're doing the best we can, all right? Everyone wants your daughter to wake up, including me. You've just got to hang in there."

Feeling suddenly disarmed, Lana nodded.

"And please leave the sensor switch alone, all right?"

Not really hearing, Lana nodded again. She was pre-occupied with the nurse's earlier words, which were echoing through her brain.

Words nobody had ever said aloud to her before.

Words that made her feel . . . quiet.

Almost calm.

As the nurse left the room, Lana folded into a chair with a sigh. In a day where so much had gone wrong, she was grateful for this one small, innocent mistake.

The nurse had called her Mrs. Cole.

22—THE ACOSTAS (AND THE PIG)

After Marissa darted off to confront her mother about moving to Ohio, the (slightly shuffled) six-pack of teens continued their trek toward the hospital. Billy was uncharacteristically quiet—silent, even—shuffling along with his pillowcase and backpack as the other teens tried to figure out what to say.

"I don't want to talk about it," Billy finally said.

Holly tried to catch his eye. "I never did, either."

Billy's focus shifted from the sidewalk to Holly as he connected the dots. Of all the people he knew, Holly was the one person who could relate.

"You can't hide it anymore," she said softly. "And that's a good thing." Then she added, "It's okay to let us in."

"It is," Dot said, maneuvering to walk beside him.

"They're right," Cricket said, moving in on his other side.

Billy took a deep breath, then glanced around at the group. "Thanks, guys."

Everyone murmured something nice, and after they'd

walked along for a little while, Casey reset the mood by saying, "If I'm not wrong, the last time Billy Pratt walked through town with a loaded pillowcase, it was Halloween."

"Dude!" Billy cried, transforming into his old self. "What a night!"

"Don't remind me!" Holly laughed, because *what a night* didn't even begin to describe it.

Billy laughed, too, then said, "You know, it's probably better if I don't haul a pillowcase into the hospital." He turned to Casey. "How about we go by your house first so I can dump this stuff?"

"Good idea," Casey said, then looked at the others. "We could meet you at the hospital."

"I'm going with you," Heather said. "I want to get rid of my backpack."

Now, Holly would have been fine with meeting them at the hospital, but Cricket and Dot were clearly in the mood to follow Billy anywhere, and after they'd also volunteered to tag along, Holly reluctantly let the teen tide sweep her to the Acostas' house.

Being a sidetrack of only two blocks, the detour should have been a short one. Especially since Casey promised to be right back as he and Billy and Heather hurried inside the house to drop their things while the others waited on the sidewalk. But (in the apparent tradition of sidetracks) there was a snag.

"Hey!" Billy called, poking his head back through the front door. "Candi says come in! There's food!"

"Candi?" Cricket asked, to which Holly replied,

"Heather's *mother*," knowing this key information would dissuade any rational being from going inside.

But then Dot said, "She's Casey's mom, too, right?" And (because Cricket didn't know Candi's role in the whole History of Nastiness) that was all Cricket needed to start up the walkway. And since *Cricket* was headed in Billy's direction, Dot followed suit, leaving Holly planted alone on the sidewalk.

"Oh, just come!" Billy called out to her with an exaggerated wave.

For most of her young life, Holly Janquell's circumstances had created a situation where she'd had no friends. And standing by herself on the sidewalk brought back the horrible feeling of being all alone in the world.

But there was Billy, waving her on, and she realized that the things she'd said to him also applied to her.

She needed to let her friends in, too.

And so (after a deep, fortifying breath) Holly unplanted herself from the sidewalk and hurried to catch up.

Now, the Acostas' house had a long (somewhat volatile) history. Inside, it had been a battleground, where fights between (and among) Acostas had raged both pre- and postdivorce, shifting over time from parent-parent to parent-teen to parent-teen-teen.

It had also been a spy zone, where Sammy and her friends had hidden in shrubbery, peeked through windows, and even infiltrated the enemy camp. Of the friends now assembled, Cricket was the only one who'd never been on (or around) the property.

But in addition to having been a battleground and spy zone, the house had also served as a retreat for Billy Pratt.

A place where he could escape.

Figure things out.

And as the three girls entered the house, it became clear that Billy wasn't the only one using it that way.

"Come in! Come in!" Mr. Acosta was saying. "How are you?" He stuck a hand out to Cricket. "I don't think we've met. I'm Warren, Casey and Heather's dad." Then he turned to the other girls and said, "Holly and Dot, am I right?"

For Holly, the complexity (and stunning weirdness) of the situation was truly beyond measure. Not only was she inside the home of the girl who'd called her a homeless hag, but she was shaking hands with Heather's curiously effusive father—who, until recently, had been living in Hollywood, head over heels in love with Sammy's mother.

How could any family recover from *that*?

So, leaving Cricket and Dot to chat with the dad, Holly cornered Casey and asked, "Your parents are back together?"

"They're taking it a day at a time," Casey whispered. "It's weird but . . . good." He grinned. "He's definitely still on the couch." Then he dropped his voice even further and added, "Look, I know you don't trust Heather, and I don't blame you. I haven't forgotten the way she treated you, or Sammy, or me for that matter. I'm just trying to give her a chance."

Suddenly Warren Acosta was next to them, and (also keeping his voice down) he asked, "How's Sammy?"

Casey gave a little shrug. "As far as we know, the same."

"Your mother and I wanted to go see her, but there's really nothing we can do, and it would probably be . . ."

His voice trailed off, so Casey nodded and finished the thought. "Awkward. Lana and Darren are dealing with a lot."

"So what's the plan?"

"Visiting hours are until eight. I think we're going to hang around there until they kick us out."

Casey's dad nodded. "Well, get something to eat before you go." He clapped a hand on his son's shoulder. "And call me. We care, you know."

So the teens gathered in the kitchen, and while Candi Acosta bustled around (in an apron and a hot mitt and high heels, no less), working the microwave as well as the oven, delivering little baked quiches and mini hotdog snacks, a revived Billy entertained the group, riffing on everything from artichokes to zombies, making even Holly laugh.

For a moment, it was as though the events at the Pratt home had never happened.

As though the battles inside the Acosta home were long forgotten.

As if no one they knew was in a coma, clinging to life.

And then, mid-bite, they heard the siren.

The wailing, urgent siren.

First in the distance, and then closer.

Right up the street.

Right there.

Mini dogs and quiches were dropped as the teens raced to the window. And when they recognized the driver of the squad car that screamed past, jaws dropped and eyes popped, and in unison the friends cried, "Let's go!"

Now, if there's one person in Santa Martina who's a wilder, faster driver than Sergeant Gil Borsch, it's Candi Acosta.

Even when she's wearing an apron and heels.

Like a streak of red lightning, she drove Casey, Heather, and a white-knuckled Holly to the hospital in her little sports car, while Warren pulled up in his sedan a good two minutes behind her with Billy, Cricket, and Dot. As fast as Candi had driven, though, she hadn't caught Sergeant Borsch. His squad car was already parked (albeit in a red zone), and he was nowhere in sight.

"Should we wait?" Warren called over to Casey as the teens bailed out of his car and raced for the hospital entrance.

"No!" Casey called back. "I'll text you!"

So as the teens disappeared inside, the Acosta adults drove away, pulling out of the hospital parking lot just as a certain bright green panel truck was pulling in.

On the drive from Sisquane, Jan DeVries had concluded that he'd been nuts to give Lucinda Huntley and her pig a lift. The last time he'd done it, a simple funeral-flower delivery had nearly become a Wild West shootout. The woman might *look* old and frail, but she was trouble.

Pig-packin' trouble.

And now that he'd picked her up (*again*) he felt responsible (*again*).

What was he going to do with her?

Or the pig?

Why hadn't he just swerved around them and kept going?

So (having given himself a stern talking-to) the burdened Dutchman parked the truck and, reminding himself that neither the pig nor the old woman was his actual responsibility, and that he was not (N-O-T) going to be persuaded to have anything to do with her quest to get a pig (a PIG!) inside a hospital, he marched around back and rolled up the door.

Lucinda was already standing.

The pig was asleep on its side.

"Thank you, young man," Lucinda said, then gave the pig a little poke with her foot. "Come along, Penny."

"Hold on a minute," Jan DeVries said. "I'm going to show you how to operate the lift gate. That way you can be in charge of your pig and your own coming and going, *ja*?"

The old woman studied him. "Still sore about the funeral? Is that it?"

"The— No! I have things here I need to do, and they do not include a pig. If you want to leave her in the truck and come with me, that's fine, *ja*? If you insist on trying to get her into the hospital, you're on your own."

"Penny's not the reason we got in trouble that day," Lucinda said carefully. She nudged the pig again. "But if that's how it's got to be, show me how to work this rig."

So the Dutchman demonstrated how to lower and raise

the lift, then tried one last time to dissuade Lucinda from bringing her pig. "If you want a ride back home, I'll be leaving in maybe half an hour."

"Don't concern yourself with me, young man. I'll be fine." Then she turned her attention to Penny, who (with some rather loud snorting) had finally gotten to her feet.

"Ma'am," Jan DeVries said (clearly exasperated), "it's going to be completely dark in a couple of hours. There's no way you can walk home."

Lucinda Huntley aimed a look at him, her eyes like the double barrels of a shotgun. "Don't tell me what I can and cannot do, and I will afford you the same courtesy." She pulled the lever, raising the lift. "Now, weren't you in some sort of hurry?"

So with a shake of his head Jan DeVries gave up. And after retrieving his sack of Dutch goodies, he locked the cab of his truck and left Lucinda Huntley and her pig to their own devices.

Whatever those might turn out to be.

23—FAIRY-TALE FANTASY

Having seen the KSMY broadcast on the Cheezers big screen, someone in the mob of teens who had not gone to Billy's house made a suggestion that got passed around and unanimously agreed upon.

It would be a tribute to Sammy!

A sign of solidarity!

And they might even get on the news.

So in flash-mob fashion, they hit the mall stores, rummaging through boxes of shoes to find their size (in fashion-forward patterns or colors, of course). Those who couldn't pay outright called their parents, pled their case, then handed their phones to the store clerks, who happily took down credit-card information. Like locusts buzzing through crops, the teens wiped out stacks of high-tops and low-cuts.

Then, with happy tummies and stylin' feet, the group (now thirty-seven in number) made its way over to the hospital with renewed energy and purpose.

Unfortunately, they were blocked at the reception desk.

"No!" one of the senior volunteers snapped, rising to his feet.

It was a new fella.

Old, and clearly ornery.

With the nametag FIG.

(That's right, FIG.)

Next to him a woman wearing the nametag BUNNY (yes, BUNNY) and sporting gray curls (which had the faint pink hue of a recent beauty-parlor treatment) rose alongside her compatriot. "No more visitors for Samantha Keyes," she said (decoding the thirty-seven-pairs-of-shoes clue). "The ICU is expelling people due to the chaos up there."

As if on cue, nearly a dozen women (all with heavy makeup, many with cheap extensions, most with Spanx-wrapped muffin tops) came from the elevator area and moved toward the exit, sniping at each other about whose fault it was that they'd been evicted (and without getting so much as a glimpse of Darren Cole).

"Barflies," Bunny grumbled as the women went past.

"They call 'em cougars these days," Fig informed her.

"Wait," one of the teens said. "You're keeping us out because of *them*?"

Fig frowned. "We're keeping you out because ICU requested it. They're overwhelmed with visitors."

"That's right." Bunny sniffed. "This is a hospital, not a zoo."

And then came a loud chorus of squawking and shrieking, followed by a distinct *snort, snort, oiiiiiiiink*.

"What *is* this?" Bunny cried as Penny and Lucinda came in, parting the sea of cougars.

"No!" Fig yelled (in a warbly, old-guy way). "There are no *pigs* allowed in here!"

"Oh, don't get your panties in a bunch," Lucinda said.

Fig's face flushed. "What?"

Lucinda ignored his indignation and clicked open her purse. "Penny has papers."

"There's no such thing as a pedigree pig!" Bunny cried. "Get that disgusting swine out of here!"

"She's a *therapy* pet," Lucinda said, unfolding a fancy certificate with blue scrolled lettering and a gold seal. "A class-A therapy pet."

"I'm warning you, ma'am," Fig said, coming out from behind the reception desk. "Remove that pig immediately."

"Let me talk to your supervisor," Lucinda said.

"First," Bunny said (also coming forward), "you take that pig and you go outside. *Then* we'll get our supervisor."

Now, while the pig situation was unfolding, the teens (who'd been standing to the side) recognized an unforeseen opportunity.

Sure, the pig standoff was funny (and tempting to watch), but the hallway to the elevator was now wide open. And the minute one of them said, "Pssst!" thirty-seven teens put their stealth moves in action, going past the reception desk, down the hallway, and into the elevator.

It was tight, but the doors did close (and giggles did erupt).

Then up, up, up they went.

Unfortunately, they were cut off at the pass by a stern-looking security guard, who wouldn't let them off the elevator. "This is not a joke," he snarled. "Go down, get out, go home."

"Yes, sir," they murmured.

But as the big steel box descended, one of them (a boy, of course) jabbed the Floor 2 button and, with a mischievous grin, asked, "Stairs, anyone?"

Now, while thirty-seven teens in high-tops were either getting cold feet or stepping out to hit the stairs, Officer Borsch was coming to grips with the reality that he'd dropped everything for a false alarm. Sammy's would-be killer was not trapped in the hallway after all.

It was just Dusty Mike.

Darren and Lana and Marko had already beat a speedy exit (courtesy of the double-shiftin' Six-strings, who showed them a back way out, down another hallway and via a different elevator, and suggested a quiet restaurant where cougars weren't known to roam). This left Hudson and Rita with Sammy-sitting duties in Room 411 (where Rita had at last relayed to Sammy—in great, excited detail—the trap and capture of the nefarious Nightie-Napper) while the rest of Sammy's friends (who'd come in just before the ICU visitor embargo was put in place) convened in the waiting room. Jan DeVries had successfully delivered his bag of Dutch treats to his daughter and was now conversing with Yolanda McKenze, while Sergeant Borsch spoke with Janet Keltner and Dusty Mike, asking questions, then answering theirs the best he could.

And while all this oh-so-serious adult stuff was going

on, something completely unrelated (and blissfully oblivious) was also taking place.

From the safety of his mother's side, Mikey McKenze was falling in love.

Likewise (from the safety of *her* mother's side), Elyssa Keltner was doing the same.

Holly was the first to notice. "Marissa!" she whispered. "Look at your brother!"

This caused the whole group to turn its attention to Mikey and Elyssa. "That is just adorable!" Dot whispered.

"Dude, she is workin' him!" Billy said.

Casey grinned. "Batty lashes."

Billy laughed, "Totally!"

"Maybe it's true love," Cricket sighed. "Maybe they'll grow up together, be best friends, fall in real love, and live happily ever after."

Which, for some reason, made the whole group go really quiet.

A sad sort of really quiet.

They were old enough to recognize when something was just a fairy tale.

Figments of love-struck imaginations.

Or . . . were they?

Marissa was the first one to have the thought, and when it came to her, her eyes popped wide open and she gasped.

She didn't *say* anything.

She just gasped.

And stared at Casey.

"What's wrong?" Dot asked.

"Yeah," Holly whispered, "why are you staring at him like that?"

"Yeah," Casey said, "why are you staring at me like that?"

And so Marissa just let it out. "You need to kiss her."

"What?" Casey asked.

Dot and Cricket caught on right away. "Oh my gosh!" they cried, then grabbed Casey's arm. "You need to kiss her!"

"Kiss her . . . *What?*"

"Kiss Sammy!" everyone (even Heather) cried.

Casey edged back. "Oh, that's . . . that's crazy!"

"No, it isn't!" Marissa said. "It's perfect! Go in there and kiss her!"

Casey shook his head. "It's not going to wake her up! She's not under some magic spell! She hit her head."

Holly frowned at him. "Well, we're going to hit *you* upside the head if you don't go in there and kiss her."

Casey stared at her, stunned.

Even *Holly* wanted him to?

"You've got to at least try!" Cricket said. "What's there to lose?"

Which *was* a compelling argument, and one Casey had no real answer to.

But what pressure!

This wasn't *Snow White* or *Cinderella* or *Sleeping Beauty* or . . . or whatever!

He wasn't some storybook prince!

A kiss wouldn't wake Sammy up!

And if he tried (and, of course, failed) everyone would be all . . . all . . . weird!

"Dude," Billy said gently, "you have to do it."

"You should *want* to do it," Marissa said.

Casey gave his friends a round of dumbfounded stares.

"Oh, just go in there and kiss her," Heather snapped. "It's not like it's gonna kill you."

So Casey let them drag him down to Room 411.

He let them convince Rita and Hudson to take a break and get a bite to eat in the cafeteria.

He let them position him at Sammy's bedside.

And then he just stood there, staring at Sammy while his friends all hovered around, holding their breath.

Waiting.

"You know what?" Heather said. "He doesn't need us staring at him. We should go."

Billy's eyes grew large. "Don't you want to see magic happen?"

"Go!" Casey snapped at him. "She's not going to wake up from me kissing her, and I don't need the pressure of you expecting magic!"

"Sorry, dude, sorry," Billy said, and Heather grabbed him by the arm and said, "Come on, let's go."

Then they all filed out, leaving Casey to make magic happen.

If he could.

24—BANISHED

I wish I could tell you that when Casey kissed Sammy, her eyes fluttered open, her heart leaped at the sight of him, and the two of them lived happily ever after.

Unfortunately, that's not what happened.

What happened was, Casey kissed Sammy (sweetly, and tenderly, and yes, on the lips), and Sammy just lay there (in the same position, eyes closed, breathing steadily).

And then Casey (poor Casey) sat down and cried.

Inside him, the sliver of hope—that fairy-tale fantasy that fights for survival in all of us—was dashed.

Banished from the Kingdom of Dreams Come True.

Maybe others saw a gauze-wrapped girl, but to him Sammy—even in this condition—was beautiful.

Much more so than Snow White or Sleeping Beauty.

Besides, he didn't want some perfect storybook character. He wanted his real-life kick-ass princess.

"Please," he begged her, "wake up."

And then (when she still didn't) he started explaining. "There is nobody like you. I know you don't think so, but it's true. Remember how we met? Well, how we met *officially*. It's not like I hadn't noticed you at school. Or heard about you from Heather." He shook his head. "Man, *nobody* stood up to Heather back then. Not even me. But you were like, *Back off, sister,* and she didn't know what to do about you.

"And you were just like that the time we had that big collision in the intersection. You had a bloody knee and a banged-up arm, and you got up and *jumped* Snake 'cause he had your skateboard. Just flew through the air, *whoosh,* and latched on to him like a cape.

"I was, like, I *love* this girl! She's fearless! And then . . . then I got to really know you. And started to really love you. Because you're so much more than just fearless. You're *real*. You're *deep*. You're smart and funny, and you care about other people. And you know what? Other people care about you. I don't think there's ever been a girl who talks back and *hits* back and takes no prisoners like you do, and then winds up with legions of fans. The whole town's after whoever did this to you.

"So it's not just me. Everyone wants you back. And maybe I'm not Prince Charming with a magic kiss, but would you wake up anyway? Please?"

Now, while Casey was pleading his case inside Room 411, outside the door the rest of the group was fidgeting, waiting for something, *anything,* to happen.

At last Holly said what they all were thinking. "It didn't work."

"Well, of course it didn't work," Heather muttered.

Not having a lot of personal experience with Heather, Cricket had no problem saying, "Hey, you thought it might, too. We all did."

"Yeah, well, we're all stupid," Heather snapped.

And Marissa was about to tell her to speak for herself when she noticed Sergeant Borsch approaching. "He's not looking too happy," she said, nodding out at the lawman.

"He never looks happy," Heather said.

Holly shrugged. "He deals with lowlifes and criminals all day."

"And us, too!" Billy threw in.

When Sergeant Borsch was upon them, Marissa asked, "Any news?"

The lawman sighed, then handed her the list she'd handed him earlier. It was now somewhat rumpled (and stained with coffee and the hydrogenated oils of a blueberry muffin), and it had notes written everywhere.

"Wait a minute," Marissa said after the teens had huddled around, studying the paper. "*Out* means they're out of jail?"

Sergeant Borsch sucked on a tooth. "That's right."

She looked at him, dumbfounded. "So it could be any of these?"

The lawman frowned and nodded. "Looks like."

"So what are you going to *do* about it?"

"We were tracking down whereabouts when there was a 911 call that the perp was cornered here in the hallway. I dropped everything and raced over. As I'm sure you heard, it was just Sammy's mother's overreaction to that Poe character."

Billy shook his head. "That dude is so misunderstood."

Sergeant Borsch tried to be diplomatic. "Well, it's understandable that he gets misunderstood."

"No, it's discrimination!" Billy said.

"Against?" Marissa asked.

Billy squared his shoulders. "Bird guys. Birdman guys. Guys who look like birds."

Sergeant Borsch pinched his eyes closed and took a deep breath. "It was *understandable* because it was an *unusual person* she didn't know in the room alone with her *daughter*. We'll just leave it at that, okay?"

Suddenly Nurse Scrabble was there, saying, "We can't have you congregating in the hall like this. I know you're all friends and this is a hard situation, but we're going to have to enforce the two-person rule. This has just gotten out of hand."

"You kids go ahead back to the waiting room," Sergeant Borsch said. "I want to see Sammy for just a minute."

"No!" Billy cried, grabbing his arm. "You can't go in there!"

The lawman cocked an eyebrow at him. "Why not?"

"Because . . ." Billy went a little shifty-eyed, but then blurted out the truth. "We want to give magic a chance."

"Magic?" Nurse Scrabble said. "What's going on in there?" But as she moved to enter Room 411, she found herself body-blocked by some very determined teens.

"It's her boyfriend," Marissa finally said.

"He's going to kiss her," Dot offered.

Nurse Scrabble stared at them a moment.

211

Then her shoulders slumped.

Her head wagged.

"Oh, you poor things," she said at last, then added, "As long as he doesn't turn off the motion sensor and climb in bed with her."

"What!?" the teens all cried, because on the surface of things it was a rather outrageous statement. Even the Borschman gave her a look.

Nurse Scrabble said, "Well, that's what the mother did. Twice! So she could get in bed with her."

Sergeant Borsch gave her a little squint. "Lana was in bed with Sammy?"

"Well, the first time. The second time she denied it."

"Denied being in bed with her?"

"No! Denied turning it off."

"Turning what off?"

"The motion sensor!"

"But she admitted it the first time?"

"How else could she have climbed in bed without the alarm going off?" Then she added, "A motion sensor doesn't just turn off by itself—you have to go over to it and switch it off!"

"But . . . how would she know where it was?" Holly asked. "Or *what* it was?"

"Yeah," Marissa said. "I had no idea there was a motion sensor."

"Where is it?" Heather asked.

"It's under the patient," the nurse said.

"But where's the switch?" Marissa asked.

"Up by the head of the bed. But the point is—"

The gears in Gil Borsch's head were visibly turning. He eyed the nurse. "Could it have been turned off beforehand?"

"Each rotation checks. And I reviewed the records when I documented that it had been turned off. It was noted as being on and functioning."

Still, for Sergeant Borsch a different sort of alarm was going off. From what the nurse was saying . . . from what he knew about Lana . . . something wasn't adding up.

"Come with me," he suddenly said to the nurse.

Nurse Scrabble clearly had no desire to do so, but Sergeant Borsch *was* an agent of the law, so she followed him to the waiting room, where the lawman led her to Dusty Mike, who was still talking to Janet Keltner.

"Mike," Sergeant Borsch began, "do you have any idea why Sammy's bed's motion sensor was turned off?"

The gravedigger gave the lawman a blank look. "What's a motion sensor?"

So (after a nod from Sergeant Borsch) Nurse Scrabble explained the setup and the purpose.

Mike shook his head. "An orderly was there when I went in. Maybe I interrupted him?"

"What was he doing?" Sergeant Borsch asked.

Dusty Mike shrugged. "Rearrangin' her pillow? That's what it looked like to me."

"Rearranging her *pillow*?" the nurse said.

Sergeant Borsch's pulse quickened. From the nurse's demeanor it was clear to him that there was no reason for anyone to be rearranging Sammy's pillow. "What did this orderly look like?" he asked Mike.

"Gold glasses. Light hair. Average size." Then he added, "The hair was a mite long."

Nurse Scrabble gave Mike a curious look. "Are you sure he was an orderly?"

He gave a little shrug. "He was wearin' scrubs."

"What color?" Gil Borsch asked.

"Blue," Dusty Mike replied.

Nurse Scrabble eyed the gravedigger suspiciously. "Hmm."

But Janet Keltner had a lot of practical experience with both medical procedure and motion sensors from her job in a nursing home and understood the need to get to the bottom of the situation. "Can I ask something?" she asked (already asking something).

"What's that?" Nurse Scrabble asked back.

"I was down in Sammy's room for a short visit while Mike was out here with my daughter. Then we switched. So between the time I left and Mike went in, an unknown orderly was in there."

"And your question is . . . ?"

"Do you have visual profiles on your personnel?"

"We do," Nurse Scrabble confirmed.

"Can he look at them?" Janet asked, nodding toward Dusty Mike.

Nurse Scrabble nodded. "Sure."

But while the others went toward the nurses' station, Sergeant Borsch headed back down the hallway, his stomach churning. He had a hunch the "orderly's" photo would not be found in the hospital's files.

"Where are you going?" Marissa asked as he passed by Room 411.

But the lawman hurried forward without a word.

If he was right, he wasn't the only one who'd been pulling a Sammy Keyes.

25—ANNIHILATING INNOCENCE

While Sergeant Borsch was headed for the exit door at the end of Sammy's hallway, the "orderly" was tearing his hair out. (And dying to tear it *off*.) Six different disguises. Six different attempts. Six different annoying, meddlesome, infuriating interferences.

So now what?

He couldn't just forget about it.

If the brat woke up, it was all over!

And there was no way he was going back to the slammer!

He stood in the stairwell, not knowing if he should go and come back later, or just wait a little while and try again. He could just kick himself for wanting her to see his face last night. For wanting her to know who was doing her in. If he'd just done the job, he wouldn't be in this predicament!

But she'd *humiliated* him.

Made his life miserable!

She needed to pay for his agonizing time in jail, but

what was the use in making her pay if she didn't know what the payback was for?

So he'd shown his face.

And he'd heard her gasp when she'd recognized him.

It had been so satisfying!

And the terror in her eyes?

Priceless.

So yes, it was worth it, but if he could go back and do it again, maybe he wouldn't worry so much about making it look like an accident. Maybe he'd just strangle her.

Or stab her.

Or shoot her!

He'd wanted to avoid evidence or noise, but now he had *this* whole mess. Which didn't seem fair. Especially since he'd been so patient and careful. So meticulous in his preparations!

After his release from jail, he'd rented two rooms. One under his real name on Boone Street, and another under a fake name at the Heavenly Hotel. The Boone Street address kept his parole officer happy. The view from his window at the Heavenly kept him happy.

It was very appropriate payback, he'd thought, to watch her from his window with binoculars. It's how he'd figured out her little jam-the-jamb trick. She thought she was so sly, but he'd verified the situation himself.

She'd used bubblegum.

And jamming the jamb and sneaking up and down the fire escape were not things you did if you were just visiting. No, she was *living* there. Illegally.

Which made her a criminal herself.

The snotty little hypocrite!

So after he'd planned and plotted and watched and let enough time pass to minimize suspicion, the embers of hatred were red-hot and he was ready to make the leap from thief to killer.

He began concealing himself in the shrubbery near the Highrise, lying in wait. Strangely, though, she seemed to stop using the stairs. Night after night he waited, but she didn't show up. And he didn't see her from his window anymore, either. Not in the morning, not in the afternoon, not in the evening.

Was she on to him?

Had she *moved*?

But then last night he'd seen her go into the Pup Parlor. And feeling a certain desperation and urgency, he'd hidden himself near the base of the Highrise stairs and waited.

And waited.

And (growing increasingly angry) waited some more.

And then suddenly there she was, stealing up the fire escape like a cat in the night.

By the third floor he'd caught her. "Remember me?" he'd asked, and he could almost feel his teeth sparkle in the moonlight. Then he'd put the muscles he'd built in the exercise yard to good use and dumped her.

But the brat had survived!

How could anyone survive that fall?

Even into bushes!

She was a living *nightmare,* and now she turned out to be Darren Cole's daughter? How could she be Darren Cole's daughter?

If he'd known *that*, he might've ransomed her instead!

But . . . her being Darren Cole's daughter made no sense. A guy like that wouldn't let his daughter live illegally at the Highrise! Well, unless he was one of those cheap millionaires who couldn't bother putting his relatives up in some classy joint.

So maybe it was a trick! Something the cops had masterminded as a way to get people to call the hotline.

Which didn't make sense, either! What would Darren Cole be doing in *Santa Martina*?

Well, at this point it didn't matter whether it made sense. What mattered was that if the girl woke up, he was dead. And the only solution was to make sure she was dead before she woke up!

And after six attempts, the best way to make that happen still seemed to be suffocation. She was already unconscious, right?

And he was *prepared*. Last night when he'd looked up how long it took to suffocate someone (because he sure didn't want to find out later that he hadn't finished the job *again*), he'd stumbled upon information on the internet about coma patients and motion sensors.

Motion sensors!

He'd had no idea.

So after reading up about those, he'd determined that all he needed was three minutes with a pillow. (The internet said it would take six, but being unconscious was like being half dead, and it's not like she'd fight back!)

Three measly minutes.

But there were always people there! First that damn cop.

The same one who'd arrested him, no less!

Then that kid who'd told him to shave.

Then the rock star, who'd thrown him by just *being* there. How could Darren Cole be two feet away from him? "Watertower" was one of his favorite songs. He'd lifted to it in the jail yard! Maybe he should have asked for an autograph. He coulda made a bundle on eBay.

Whatever. The second time he saw Darren Cole, he'd stayed cool and collected, and getting him to leave the room would have been easy if it hadn't been for the mom (who made it more than clear who the brat took after).

There were also those nuns who he'd *thought* were there because she'd died on her own, but oh, no. She wouldn't do him the courtesy of just *dying*.

And then there was that weird bird-looking guy who'd appeared out of nowhere and had scared the hell out of him.

Six tries and he still couldn't get three measly minutes? It wasn't fair!

So there he stood, in the safety of the stairwell, brooding, trying to decide how long he needed to wait before trying again, wondering if he should switch disguises *again,* when he heard a click. A loud click. Followed by the unmistakable *whoosh* of the door on the level above.

As silently and quickly as he could, he started down the steps. And he would have just flown down the levels to the first floor and out of the stairwell, but on the level below him there was another loud click.

And another *whoosh.*

And lots of whispering voices.

Panic swelled inside him. Were people after him? Was he trapped?

And then he heard a voice on the level above.

A voice he recognized.

When Gil Borsch pushed the stairway exit door open, the first place he looked was the doorjamb.

Sure enough, the latch-plate hole had something crammed inside it.

A napkin, folded up into a hard, stiff wad.

"Kids!" he called over to the teens standing outside Sammy's room. "Don't let anyone in there you don't know!" And then he was gone, pounding down the stairs.

His mind ran down the List. The possibilities.

Garnucci was locked up in jail, so it couldn't be him. Of the others who were out of jail, one stuck in his mind as the clear choice because criminals tended to repeat their MO.

Like the use of disguises.

And wadded napkins.

Which had both been used previously by only one of the criminals on the List.

Sammy had trapped the lowlife in true Sammy style—by pinning him half inside a Dumpster and then jumping up and down on the lid to keep him from escaping. He'd never heard a man yelp (or curse) like that before (or since). When they'd finally extracted him from the Dumpster, he was covered in trash and slime.

And mad as a hornet!

Now, while Gil Borsch was moving down the stairs (as fast as his composition and coordination would allow) with all of this flashing through his mind, the "orderly" had run into an unexpected situation that was potentially worse than trying to get past a cop without being recognized.

What the orderly faced was not hospital personnel taking a shortcut out of the building.

What he faced was a group of kids.

Teenagers.

And when he saw the shoes, he knew.

This was trouble.

But suddenly he was struck with a very clever idea.

"Hey," he said, smiling through the bullets that were sweating past his wig. "Your friends are waiting for you up on Four. The door's open."

The teens (who'd been ditching unfriendly hospital staff left and right and were down from thirty-seven to seventeen in number) were surprised to find themselves not only not busted, but *helped* by an orderly. "Thanks, man!" they said, and while they began pounding up the stairs, the escape artist caught the closing Floor 2 door and slipped inside.

Which left Sergeant Gil Borsch roadblocked by seventeen teens in high-tops.

Now, at one time, this would have caused the lawman to have a coronary.

Or perhaps a stroke.

Or (more likely) both.

But something had changed in Gil Borsch. Something for the better.

Based on the shoes, these were clearly friends of

Sammy's. So instead of asking them what they thought they were doing, messing around on the hospital stairs, he asked, "Did you see anybody on the stairwell? A guy in blue scrubs?"

"Yeah!" a girl in the group answered. "He went through the door we came out of."

"What floor?"

"Two!"

"How long ago?"

"Just now. He told us to go up to Four. That our friends were waiting for us."

"Clever," the Borschman grumbled, then said, "Guys, I need your help."

And the teens (doubly surprised to be recruited by a cop after fleeing dozens of people in a variety of uniforms) simply held still and said, "Sure."

"Go up to Four. Tell your friends about the guy you just saw. He isn't a real orderly. I think he's the one who hurt Sammy, and I'm pretty sure his name's Larry Daniels."

"Larry Daniels?"

"Otherwise known as Oscar the Ice Cream Man."

"An *ice cream man* tried to kill her?" someone cried.

"That's just *wrong*," another teen added.

And then came a fast and furious exchange inside the group.

"Dude, my fragile innocence has been annihilated!"

"Shut up! This is serious!"

"I *am* serious!"

"Yeah! Who doesn't trust the ice cream man?"

"Oh, right. When have you ever seen an ice cream man?"

"In the movies?"

"No, really! There used to be that guy on Broadway? Remember him?"

"Stop it!" Sergeant Borsch cried as he muscled forward. "Just go up there and tell them! Please!"

"Dude," the kid with the annihilated innocence said as the lawman went by, "you sound like you're planning to die or something."

"Just tell them!" the lawman begged.

Then he pushed through the teens and hurried down the stairs.

26—THE CHASE

Up on the fourth floor, Casey Acosta could hear a commotion outside of Room 411. And (still talking to his kickass sleeping beauty) he interrupted himself to tell Sammy, "Something's going on out there. I'm gonna go check." And since he was holding her hand, he kissed it and said, "I'll be right back."

But no sooner had he stood and turned than he heard, "Case."

It was so quiet that it might have been from outside the room . . . only it had come from behind him.

He whipped around and there she was, wrapped in gauze, plumbed with tubes and wires and . . . awake!

"Sammy!" he cried, then spun around twice not knowing what to do first. "Sammy!" he cried again, then held up a finger. "Wait a minute! Wait a minute! I'll be right back!" He raced to the door, flung it open, and yelled, "She's awake!" then raced back to her side. His eyes were burning with tears as he grabbed her hand. "You're awake!"

She gave him a weak smile, but instead of saying anything, her smile drifted away.

"What's wrong?" Casey asked, shifting from euphoric to panicked.

"Oscar pushed me," she whispered. "Did they catch him?"

Casey had no idea who Oscar was, but his phone was out in a flash and he was calling Sergeant Borsch. "She's awake," Casey said when the lawman answered. "She says it was Oscar. Do you know who that is?"

"We're on his tail now," Gil Borsch replied. And then (with a voice that could only be described as choked up) he said, "Give her a kiss for me," and hung up.

So Casey delivered the kiss to Sammy's forehead, saying, "That's from the Borschman. He says they're on his tail now!" He hesitated, then said, "Who's Oscar?"

"The Ice Cream Man? The Hotel Thief?"

"That guy you *waved* at?"

She nodded. "That's the one."

Casey shook his head. There was so much he wanted to ask her. So much he wanted to *tell* her. Like about what everyone was doing to try to help. Like about the List.

So much had happened!

But first he got busy with his phone again. "I need to tell your grandmother and Hudson! And your mom and dad! They've been going nuts."

"How long was I out?" Sammy asked, testing her arms and legs.

"Forever! Uh, I mean, almost twenty-two hours? Something like that."

"Really?"

He nodded as he waited for the ringing line to be answered. "Do you feel okay? What hurts?"

She gave him a small grin. "Uh, everything?"

Casey's attention snapped to the phone. "She's awake!" he said. "She seems to be fine! . . . Yes . . . Yes . . . I don't know . . . Sure! . . . Can you call Lana and Darren?" And when he got off the phone, he grinned at Sammy and said, "They'll be right here. With your parents, I'm sure. And Marko!"

"Marko's here?" she asked. But then she began blinking and turned away. Like she was trying to remember something.

"What's wrong?" Casey asked. "Are you all right?"

"Was . . . was Dusty Mike here?"

Casey's eyes popped wide. "Yes!"

Sammy kept blinking. "Oh . . . wow." She looked at him. "And you . . . you kissed me?"

"Yes!"

"And cried . . . ?"

"Yes!"

"And my . . . my mom? She was . . ." She looked over at where Lana had slept, and tears filled her eyes. "It's like a dream. Like an invisible movie." She blinked some more as she wiped away her tears. "Wow."

"So you remember . . . ?"

She looked around. "Marko singing about teddy bears?"

"I hadn't heard about that one! But these bears *were* Marko's idea." He handed one to her. "Everyone wrote on the ribbons."

"Oh!" Sammy said, reading. "This is awesome!"

When she reached for another bear, Casey said, "I need to go tell Marissa. And Holly and Dot! And Heather!"

"And Billy?"

"Billy! Right! I wonder where they went."

And he was about to run up to the waiting room (where he was sure their friends had been banished) when Nurse Scrabble walked in. "I *did* hear correctly!" she said, grinning. "Hello, Samantha! Glad to have you back with us. How are you feeling?"

"Really strapped down," she said, looking at all the tubes and wires. "Can we get rid of this stuff?"

"Let me get the doctor in here," she said, checking the machines over. "But I'm pretty sure we can make that happen."

"Can you tell our friends in the waiting room that she's awake?" Casey asked.

"Uh, no."

"No?"

"They all took off. Which was good because they were loud and rambunctious and I have no idea how that new batch got past the sign-in desk."

"Do you know where they went?"

"I heard them say something about catching the ice cream man." She laughed and shook her head. "When's the last time you've seen an ice cream man?"

"Last night," Sammy said. "When he tried to kill me."

Nurse Scrabble's eyebrows went flying. "What?"

Sammy shrugged. "Well, you're right. He's not actually

an ice cream man. That was just his cover—a blind ice cream man."

"A *blind* ice cream man? This story keeps getting stranger and stranger." Nurse Scrabble shook her head. "But let me get the doctor so he can let you know what to expect."

Now, as badly as Sammy might have wanted to get out of the hospital, there was one person who wanted out more:

Larry Daniels.

Also known as the formerly blind ice cream man.

Or the disorderly orderly.

After narrowly escaping Sergeant Borsch, Larry Daniels had ripped off his wig and fake glasses and stuffed them in a laundry hamper on Floor 2, and was now proceeding (as nonchalantly as he could) along the corridor of the maternity wing to the elevator. In a test of both patience and acting ability, he politely fielded two requests (one for changing linens, another for restocking toilet paper) before blithely continuing his trek toward the elevator.

Unfortunately for the formerly blind ice cream man, when the elevator door opened he came face to face with a mob of teenagers.

And recognized some of their faces.

It was the same group he'd seen in the stairwell!

Doubly unfortunately for the formerly blind ice cream man, there were a few extra teens in the mob.

One who recognized *him*.

Marissa (who had also witnessed the Dumpster Incident) pointed and cried, "That's him!"

And with that simple statement, the chase was on.

The problem was, the good guys looked like bad guys (they were teenagers running and shouting through a maternity ward, after all), and the bad guy (still dressed as a hospital worker) looked like the good guy.

"Stop him!" the teens cried as he bolted back toward the stairs.

"Stop them!" the would-be murderer cried as he threw carts and laundry hampers in their path.

"Call security!" a nurse cried as she was bowled over by teens in high-tops.

"What security?" another nurse cried, because, really, what security?

"Whaaaa!" the babies in the ward cried, because, well, that's what babies do.

Now, had Sergeant Borsch been able to enter the Floor 2 stairwell door, he would most certainly have done so in pursuit of Larry Daniels.

But there was no wadded napkin in the Floor 2 doorjamb, and by the time he'd reached it, it was latched up tight.

So he hustled down to the first floor and used the exterior exit (where he discovered another folded-up napkin). Then out he went, radioing the station as he hustled around the building to the front of the hospital, calling for backup and requesting an APB for one Larry Daniels.

In a fair world, Sergeant Gil Borsch would have been rewarded for his stalwart determination and commitment with a bit of good luck. But, as we all know, it's not a fair world, and luck, in Gilbert Borsch's corner of this unfair world, is not something that shows itself very often.

(Or, really, ever.)

So it should have been no surprise to him that the first "backup" to appear on the scene was a self-proclaimed superhero roaring into the parking lot on his High Roller with a fortune-teller in the sidecar.

"Commissioner!" Justice Jack cried. "Which way did he go?"

"I can't believe it's that same creep!" Madame Nashira cried from the sidecar (as she had been one of Larry Daniels's past victims). "I'll rip his eyes out!"

From his Saddle of Justice, Jack looked at the fortune-teller and a little red heart practically popped out of his chest and floated dreamily above him.

"Why me?" the lawman moaned.

And, as if dealing with Justice Jack and his new fortune-telling sidekick weren't enough, the unfortunate lawman was suddenly (and rudely) goosed.

By a pig.

"Hey!" he squawked as he jumped, and when he turned around, Penny oinked at him (loud and long and lovingly).

"No!" the lawman screamed, backing away. "What are *you* doing here?" Because, yes, he knew Penny. And yes, Penny remembered him, too. And it was undeniable— Penny was still very much an oinker in love.

"Stay back!" he commanded as Penny approached. "Do you hear me? Stay back!"

Now, if a pig could coo, that's what Penny would have been doing.

But pigs can't coo.

They can only oink.

And snort.

And kind of snotter.

And since Sergeant Borsch was distracted by Penny oinking madly and frolicking after him, and since Justice Jack and Madame Nashira were likewise distracted *watching* Penny oink and frolic, neither the crime fighters nor the claw-wielding fortune-teller noticed the two swarms of teens approaching.

From one side came Marissa and her group, still chasing Larry Daniels after they'd tailed him down the back stairs.

From the other side came the other (newly text-alerted) teens, who had opted *not* to take the stairs (and had been evicted by Fig and Bunny).

And, chalk it up to bad luck or good fortune, but it does seems fitting that the formerly blind ice cream man/wannabe kid killer would be tackled by kids.

Loud, angry kids who knew how to apply a hammerlock and grind a cheek into asphalt.

"You thought you'd get away with it?" they crowed as they brought him down. "You mess with Sammy, you mess with all of us!"

"Yeah! You're going away for good, dude! You are toast!"

And then over his shoulder, Billy cried, "Officer Borsch! Get over here! Cuff this guy!"

For Larry Daniels, it wasn't the pain of the hammerlock or the little road rocks being ground into his cheek.

It wasn't the metal cuffs ratcheting around his wrists or the sound of a cop reading him his rights again. It wasn't even the pig that came from God-knows-where to sniff and snort and slobber around his head.

It was the shoes.

All he could see was those shoes.

Shoes that were just like hers.

Shoes that would give him nightmares for the rest of his life.

GOODBYE

It's never easy to say goodbye.

Well, unless it's a good-riddance sort of goodbye, and then it's super easy.

But when you love someone and it's time . . . well, it's hard.

Really, really hard.

It does help knowing that they're going to be okay, and Sammy *is* going to be okay. You should have seen the commotion on the fourth floor. Everybody was there, and you know what? The hospital just let them invade. After all, it's smart to be agreeable when questions of slipshod security could develop into lawsuits. Plus, it's a well-known fact that keeping celebrities happy is sound business practice.

The invasion started with Rita, who skidded up to the bed in her high-tops and then sobbed happy tears until Sammy told her, "Grams! Stop it! I'm fine!"

Hudson, too, was reduced to happy tears, and then came Lana and Darren and Marko, followed by a seemingly endless stream of friends.

They did draw the line at Penny, but after Lucinda was reunited with her love-struck pig and learned that Sammy was no longer in need of pet therapy, the old woman gave her stubborn streak a rest and accepted a ride home from Mr. DeVries.

So in Room 411 there were lots of hugs and kisses and laughter (and a very emotional reconciliation between Lana and Rita), and although some people stayed to just deliver a quick high five (or, in the case of Justice Jack, a quick "Justice prevails, young firecracker!"), there were those who, once in the room, wouldn't budge.

People like Rita and Hudson.

And Lana and Darren and Marko.

And Marissa and Holly and Billy and Dot.

Even Cricket.

And Heather.

And, of course, Casey.

The room was filled with the chattering of voices and the sharing of bears and the retelling of stories and just . . . joy. Somehow the scrappy girl who'd had practically no family and only one friend the first time she'd tangled with Larry Daniels had a whole city rallying around her.

She was surrounded by family.

Surrounded by friends.

Surrounded by love.

It was easy to see, she was going to be *fine*.

Still, it was hard to leave. Even after word came down that she wouldn't be discharged until the next day and the hospital shooed everyone away, even after the parking lot was quiet and darkness had fallen, it was hard to leave.

Hard for *me* to say goodbye.

Outside, I lingered in the parking lot, trying to figure

out which window was hers. The fourth floor about . . .
there. Then I just stood under a streetlamp, and watched
as the windows went dark, one by one, waiting for hers to
go dark, too, so I could say good night.

And goodbye.

But instead of her light going off, suddenly there she
was, at the window.

I watched her as she looked out, looked around, obviously thinking.

And as I watched her, *I* couldn't help but think of the
way she's changed *my* life. The way she's made me laugh,
and grow, and feel. The way that she's helped me see that
a good heart and a strong head will take you anywhere you
want to go. The way she's lifted me through dark times
and, probably most of all, the way she's been a friend.

A real friend.

Lost in thought, I hadn't noticed that her position had
shifted, that she was looking more downward.

That she seemed to be looking at . . . me.

Could she really be looking at . . . me?

"Sammy," I whispered as I put my hand to my heart.

She just stood there, still, staring at . . . me?

So I blew her a kiss, and that's when she did something
that caught me by surprise, although it probably shouldn't
have. Something that made me know that she will always
be the feisty, fearless, and funny girl I love.

She waved.

What do you think?

A few questions for you or your book club to ponder.

Sammy feels like an outsider at the beginning of seventh grade in *Sammy Keyes and the Hotel Thief*. But now, at the end of eighth grade, when she's in trouble, loads of people are there to help. Do you think that would surprise Sammy? Did it surprise you?

Do you think Sammy has changed over the past two years? If so, in what ways?

And how have all the people around her evolved? Think of Grams and Hudson, Marissa and Heather. And what about Lady Lana—has she grown too?

How is Sammy responsible for changing other people's lives? Think about Holly. And Officer Borsch. And what about you? Has Sammy changed your life in any way?

Over the course of the series, Sammy helps a lot of people. Which characters are your favorites? Gina the fortune-teller? Lucinda and her pet pig? Justice Jack?

Sammy's made new friends, but she's also made a few enemies. Who are your favorite bad guys?

Do you have a favorite Sammy Keyes book? Why that one? Which book was funniest? Scariest? Most mysterious? Most romantic? If you could pick one book in the series to be in alongside Sammy, which would it be, and which character would you like to be?

Sammy and Marissa's friendship gets tested a few times, but they always seem to find a way to work it out. What makes them such good friends?

Casey seems to like Sammy as soon as he meets her. But Sammy's a little slower to admit that she might like him. Did you like how their relationship evolved over many books? What are your three favorite Sammy and Casey moments?

On the other hand, Heather seems to loathe Sammy as soon as she meets her! These two do terrible things to each other. Do you have a favorite Heather moment? Which payback felt the most satisfying to you?

Wendelin Van Draanen wrote this final book in the series in a very different way than the rest. Since Sammy's unconscious, she can't tell her own story! So here Wendelin herself becomes the narrator. Did you like seeing all the characters Sammy's described through this new lens? Do you think this was a good way to say goodbye?

This story reminds us just how many people's lives Sammy has impacted over the course of two years. Think of your own life. Has someone new come into your life and made a difference? Do you think you've made a difference in someone else's life?

Are there ways you are like Sammy? Would you like to be her? Or to have her as a friend?

What's the thing you will remember most about the Sammy Keyes series?

Sometimes we're in such a hurry to find out what happens that we miss the little things on a quick read through a book. Now that you've read all of the Sammy Keyes books, do you think you would enjoy them in a new way by reading them again? If so, where would you want to start? Back at the beginning with Sammy's first wave or . . . ?

Did you know that you can read about Holly's life *before* she meets Sammy Keyes?

Check out her story in *Runaway*.

FROM THE AUTHOR OF *FLIPPED*

Wendelin Van Draanen

RUNAWAY

10:30 at night

I've got to get out of Aaronville. This is a podunk little town, and I swear everybody's giving me the who-are-you-and-where's-your-mother look.

Dead, you morons! Dead!

I hate that look because it reminds me.

Plus, it usually means the police'll come sniffing around.

So, Holly, you ask, it's ten-thirty at night . . . are you back in the bushes?

Are you crazy? Am I wasting battery power writing this with my flashlight on?

No chance!

Or as my mother would say, "No chance in France!"

She always wanted to go to France. And when she talked about it, she'd always wind up singing some song about breaking through to the other side.

Break on through to the other side,

Break on through to the other side . . .

Have you ever heard that song? There were more words, but that's all I remember.

Crud. I've got to stop talking about my mom. What I was telling you about is where I am, which is inside Aaronville's *other* fast food joint. There's no salad bar here, but when I scoped out the place where I went last night, that same manager guy was walking around the dining area, so I came here instead.

That's the pain about being a gypsy child instead of a gypsy adult. People call the cops a lot quicker.

But it turns out that this place has a great dollar menu. And since I was all out of Camille's cafeteria food, I broke down and spent my first buck. I ordered a double cheeseburger, and when I asked if veggies were extra, the girl who rang me up said, "Nah." So I asked for pickles and onions and lettuce and tomatoes. "Lots!" I told her.

She looked at me like I was a dweeb, and when my burger arrived, it had about six inches of veggies on it. I suspect they were making fun of me, because the place is pretty dead and they don't seem to have much to do, but the joke's on them. I took all the veggies off, got a little plastic fork and knife and a few mayo packets, cut the mayo into the veggies, tossed it all with salt and pepper, and *mm-mmm.* One delicious *free* salad.

So I'm down a dollar, but I still have half the burger, which I'll save for breakfast. It's cold enough outside to keep it from rotting, but I hope it doesn't attract bears. Though I doubt there are bears in

Aaronville. Dogs, sure. But if one of them comes sniffing around, I'll share.

So you want to know what I did all day?

Well, I'm not going to go into a ton of detail because I don't want to waste my whole night writing again, but basically, I went into the library, where I used the bathroom, read the paper, got quizzed up by a librarian (I told her I was homeschooled and that I was doing an assignment), "borrowed" a paperback book that looked pretty good (but wasn't), read the whole thing out in the sunshine at a park (which was really more like a strip mall of grass), walked to the outskirts of town, and discovered (*ta-da*) train tracks!

And guess what?

They run east-west!

Oh, crud. Those same goth kids from last night just came in and spotted me.

They're looking at me and whispering.

And evil-goth-kid laughing.

I'm out of here.

May 26th, 10 a.m.

There are probably only four goth kids in this whole podunk town, and of course their idea of fun is terrorizing the town's only gypsy. Too bad for them I've got a lot of experience ditching people: goth kids, cops, store managers, pizza delivery boys. . . . The way I do it is, I cut and run, then I hide and hold.

It's the "holding" part that's hard. Even five minutes of holding still seems like an eternity, but you've got to make yourself do it for at *least* half an hour. It's the key to getting away. If you come out too early, you'll get caught, guaranteed.

The goth kids were plenty ticked off when I lost them. I could hear them shouting at each other, "She went this way!" "No, dude, *this* way!"

I held still for like an *hour* before finally going back to the library bushes, but the whole thing made me jumpy. I didn't sleep very well at all. I woke up about twenty times.

And since I'd already overstayed my unwelcome in Aaronville, I packed up early this morning, ate my half-a-burger, and hiked down to the town's 7-Eleven, which I'd walked past the day before.

I waited for the prework rush, when all 7-Elevens (even the one in Aaronville) get busy. I had a mental list already made: pop-top cans of meat, protein bars, and Gatorade. No filler food like candy and cookies—Spam will take you a lot farther than Oreos.

I'm sure you've noticed that 7-Elevens have shoplifting mirrors and cameras everywhere, but I've learned about timing and positioning and how to avoid getting caught. And in all the food runs I've made (which I'm sure you'll be horrified to learn is way more than I can remember), I've only been busted once.

I bit my way out of that one.

Anyway, I went into the 7-Eleven, keeping the rules of lifting in the front of my mind: Find the mirrors. Find the employees. Act normal. Don't linger. Don't dart your eyes around. Don't get greedy. Be smooth.

I also attached myself to an adult, without getting so close that she noticed. She made for great cover as I slipped things into my jacket pockets.

The last rule is: Buy something. You've got to, or why'd you come in?

So I stood in line with all the rush-hour people and bought myself a pack of gum. Sugar-free peppermint. When you run out of food, it really helps with the hunger pangs.

Then I walked out and hiked to the outskirts of town, and now I'm down at the railroad tracks.

Waiting.